S0-ACP-849

She was trembling from that last kiss. Her body tingled with desire, refusing to calm down. It craved release from the tension and unsatisfied sexual frustration strumming through it. She hated to think what would have happened if he hadn't got that phone call. It was becoming increasingly difficult to resist Phillip, but she had to somehow find the strength to keep on doing it until she left Magnolia Grove. She had only a few days to go, but they would be the longest ones she would ever have to endure. God, help her she wanted to give in and let him make love to her. She knew it would go beyond physical satiation between them; even beyond rapture.

BEYOND THE RAPTURE

BEVERLY CLARK

Genesis Press Inc.

Indigo Love Stories

An imprint of Genesis Press Inc.
Publishing Company

Genesis Press, Inc.
P.O. Box 101
Columbus, MS 39703

All rights reserved. Except for use in any review, the reproduction or utilization of this work in whole or in part in any form by any electronic, mechanical, or other means, not known or hereafter invented, including xerography, photocopying and recording, or in any information storage or retrieval system, is forbidden without written permission of the publisher, Genesis Press, Inc. For information write Genesis Press, Inc., P.O. Box 101, Columbus, MS 39703.

All characters in this book have no existence outside the imagination of the author and have no relation whatsoever to anyone bearing the same name or names. They are not even distantly inspired by any individual known or unknown to the author and all incidents are pure invention.

Copyright© 2005 by Beverly Clark

ISBN: 1-58571-130-6
Manufactured in the United States of America

First Edition

Visit us at www.genesis-press.com
or call at 1-888-Indigo-1

cles on Lily's hospital bed.

"The doc and his family are loaded. They own a multimillion-dollar construction and architectural business."

"Then what's he doing working here?"

"Don't ask me." He frowned curiously. "Why are you so interested in him? You got the hots for the good doctor or something?"

"Carey!"

"I was just asking."

"I talked to Mimi and she won't let me come to work until Dr. Cardoneaux releases me."

"So?"

"He won't until he's satisfied that I'm sufficiently recovered. According to him, I'm nowhere near to being well. That's the reason he invited me to recuperate at his family estate."

"Whatever you say," he agreed, then in the next breath said, "Maybe he has the hots for you."

"It's not like that, Carey."

"You sure?"

Ignoring him, Lily thumbed through one of the magazines he'd gotten for her. She gasped when she came to a picture of Magnolia Grove. It looked like one of the plantation mansions in *Gone with the Wind*. Did he really live there? Why would he suggest that she convalesce there? Could Carey be right about the doctor's true intentions? She couldn't picture his southern, white aristocratic family agreeing to let a strange black woman come live in their house. What was really behind his offer? She had to wonder.

"Mother, I'm expecting a houseguest, who should be arriving, in a couple of days," Phillip said as he entered the breakfast room.

"A houseguest?" she said nearly spilling her coffee

"Yes. Would you have one of the guest suites readied?"

"Surely you haven't invited one of your patients to stay here?"

"As a matter of fact I have." He walked over to the buffet to serve himself. "She's a model that has worked herself to the point of collapse and needs rest, quiet and good food to properly recover her health. I knew that Magnolia Grove would be the ideal place to do that so I invited her to stay and recuperate. She hasn't given me her answer, but I expect her to accept my invitation."

"Phillip. You don't know anything about this woman."

"I know all I need to. If it's going to be a problem for you—"

"I didn't say that. What is this woman's name?"

Phillip smiled. He could almost see the wheels turning in his mother's head. Before the day was over she will have found out everything there is to know about Lily Jordan.

"Mother, this is Phillip you're talking to. I know how your mind works. I don't want you playing detective."

"But, Phillip—"

"I mean it mother. You leave my patient to me. If I want to know about her background, I'll ask her."

"In other words cease and desist."

"You're a quick study. But the point is, are you going to do as I asked?"

"Are you giving me any other choice?"

Phillip kissed his mother's cheek and left for the hospital.

Lily waited until the nurse finished taking her pulse to ask her a question.

"What do you know about Dr. Cardoneaux?"

"Like what?"

"I read in a magazine that his family owns a multimillion-dollar business. And the picture of his house really impressed me. It made me wonder why he works in a city hospital."

The nurse smiled. "I used to wonder the same thing myself. He's thirty-three. And gorgeous, isn't he? He certainly seems interested in you. I can tell the feeling is mutual.

Lily ignored the last part of her comment. "About Dr.

Cardoneaux."

"Well, he's single. And completely dedicated to his work. He could have gone into one of those exclusive upscale private practices, but he enjoys helping people less fortunate then himself."

"The article I read said he is well loved by his patients."

"He is that all right. Around here, we call him the young miracle worker. Believe me, all us single girls have tried to snag his attention. Even a few who aren't single." She cleared her throat. "You seem to be coming along fine, Ms. Jordan. You look more rested. I'll note that on the chart. Dr. Phil is a stickler for details. He believes in treating the whole patient."

Lily watched the nurse leave and then lay back against the pillow. The staff certainly loved the good doctor. And from the way Nurse Alice Clayborne spoke of him he had earned her respect. Well, at least he was a good doctor even if as a man he was as aggravating as hell. Still she wondered what made him decide to work in a city hospital considering his privileged background.

Phillip waited a few minutes outside Lily Jordan's room before going in. He was anxious to know the answer to his offer to stay at Magnolia Grove, but he was not sure he would be happy about her decision.

"Well, what is it to be, Ms Jordan?" he asked entering her room.

"I'll agree under one condition."

"And that is?"

"That I meet your mother first."

He frowned. "Why would you think you needed to do that?"

"I don't need to. But I'm sure it's not every day you invite a black person to stay in your ah man—house."

Phillip smiled. So that's what she thought; of course she didn't know that he was also the product of a mixed heritage. Evidently, thinking he was white bothered her. Had she had a bad experience with a white man and wanted nothing to do with any of them? She was part white. Could she possibly have turned her back on that side of her heritage? If so, he wondered about her background. It was ironic. It wasn't that long ago that his mother had confessed to being part black and turning her back on that side of her heritage. Going so far as to block it out entirely.

"All right. I'll introduce you to my mother. My brother doesn't live with us so that introduction will have to wait until another time." He cleared his throat. "The chart says you ate a healthy breakfast."

"There wasn't much they could do to ruin cold cereal, orange juice and fruit."

"I promise you, you'll enjoy the food where you'll be going a lot more. Trust me."

"I don't know if I should, considering that you slipped that sedative into my juice."

"I wouldn't have had to resort to that if you'd been more cooperative. You need to stay in the hospital for at least another day. Then I'll take you to Magnolia Grove. What about clothes?"

"I'll have a friend pack a suitcase for me."

"Is Mr. Graham that friend?"

Lily smiled. "Actually no. I do have other friends, believe it or not."

"I didn't mean to imply— Do you have to take offense at everything I say?"

"I don't."

"Oh, yes you do. Look, I have rounds to make. I'll be in early tomorrow morning, then we'll drive out to Magnolia Grove."

CHAPTER FOUR

"The first Andre Cardoneaux, my great great-grandfather immigrated from France to the United States and bought Magnolia Grove in the 1700's. Many years later, my Grandfather share cropped all but fifty of the five thousand acres during the 1930's depression. And my father sold all but fifty acres to start Cardoneaux Construction. When my brother Nicholas joined the business, the architectural firm was added."

"You were never interested in joining them?" Lily asked Phillip.

"Oh no. Since I was seven years old I knew that I wanted to be a doctor. I left the running of the business strictly to my father and brother."

"You said you live at Magnolia Grove with your mother.

Are your parents divorced?"

"No, my father died five years ago in a yachting accident."

"I'm sorry, I didn't meant to—"

"You had no way of knowing. My father was a bit of a traditionalist in that he expected my brother and me to live at Magnolia Grove and raise our children there and pass on the Cardoneaux legacy through them as his father had through him. Unfortunately these days tradition isn't always strictly adhered to. Nicholas decided to move into a house he designed and had built. I could have moved out too, but Mother would have been alone in that big house, and since I was single I stayed." Phillip smiled. "We've arrived."

Lily gazed around her in amazement as they drove through a magnificent alley of Oak trees leading up to the mansion. She had done photo shoots in places similar to this, but never stayed in one as a guest.

Phillip could tell that she was impressed with his home. Now if his mother only behaved herself. Despite what had happened between her and his brother, she was still overprotective and tended to maneuver things in the direction she thought they should go. She was basically a southern aristocrat to the soles of her feet.

Phillip got out of the car and came around to the passenger side to help Lily, then escorted her to the front door of the house. Edwards, the Cardoneaux's new butler, met them. Their old one had recently retired.

"Mrs. Cardoneaux is waiting for you in the living room, sir."

"Thank you, Edwards."

The butler directed them into the living room, then discreetly took his leave.

Lily couldn't believe any of this. The Cardoneaux's actually had a butler! It was like stepping back in time or looking in on the set of a civil war movie. She was curious as well as anxious to meet Phillip's mother.

"Mother, I'd like you to meet, Lily Jordan. Lily, Suzette Cardoneaux."

"Pleased to meet you, Mrs. Cardoneaux." Lily extended her hand.

She shook the proffered hand in a quick limp contact of palms. "So you're my son's newest project."

Phillip flinched. He would definitely have to have a serious conversation with his mother. She wasn't exactly rude, but she was far from welcoming.

"I'll have Edna bring in some coffee. If you'll excuse me, Ms. Jordan." Suzette smiled politely. "Edwards will put your suitcases in the east wing guest suite." With that she left them alone.

"You have a beautiful home, Dr. Cardoneaux. Look, if it's too much of an imposition you don't have to let me stay."

"It's not. And I insist on it. Please, call me Phillip."

"But your mother—"

"Is a snob, but she's really harmless. Once she gets to know you—"

"She'll be friendlier towards me? I doubt that. But I'll stay for a few days."

"No, two weeks at least. You'll need every bit of that time to regain your strength, Lily."

Lily had met women like Suzette Cardoneaux. In fact the woman reminded her of her Aunt Margaret. She could handle her. Magnolia Grove was what really interested her.

And Dr. Phillip Cardoneaux doesn't?

He did she had to admit. But that was all.

"All right, I'll stay, doctor. Right now I'm too tired to argue about how long."

"Good. I'll take you to your suite."

As they walked through the house, Lily was awed by the rich antique furnishings and plush carpeting in the rooms. And the gilt-framed pictures that lined the walls in the hall. She wondered if they were of his ancestors.

"Here we are." Phillip opened a heavy, oak wood beautifully hand-carved door.

Lily had never stayed in a hotel that was any more elegant.

"This has all the comforts of an apartment; complete with a small kitchen and sitting room," he said walking through as he spoke.

As they entered the bedroom, Phillip opened the door to a huge Roman styled ivory and gold veined marble bathroom that made her moan inwardly at the thought of bathing in such luxury. There were bottles of expensive bath oils and lotions. On one wall a rack of huge cream-colored Turkish towels.

Phillip cleared his throat and smiled, then indicated a terraced garden beyond the French doors and walked over and opened them. "That path leads to the swimming pool and jacuzzi. Then beyond that is a tennis court and also a golf course."

"Definitely all the comforts of home."

Phillip frowned. Had he overwhelmed her? He knew that not many people enjoyed the luxuries he'd taken for granted all his life. He and his brother Nicholas's friend, Henri and his wife Jolie and their two children lived in the apartment above his art gallery in the French Quarter. He remembered when they were boys how he and Nicholas had escaped their mothers' overprotective, social-conscious eyes, caught the streetcar and gone to visit Henri and his family. They lived in a small, but comfortable house near Treme.

The color scheme carried throughout the guest suite was apricot, muted oranges, beige and creams. Creamy beige Persian carpet covered the bedroom floor. The walls were painted peach with apricot organza curtains at the windows. On the French provincial bed was a satin spread done in a warm orange floral print with Ivory-cream colored eyelet lace trim to match the covering on the sheets and pillows.

Lily was beyond impressed by her surroundings. Her father had once told her that his family had owned a plantation in Georgia that had survived the civil war only to be sold in the early 60s. She wondered if he ever thought about what it had been like and missed living there. He rarely ever spoke about it. But then he'd been too busy quarreling with her mother about other things. Those particular memories from her childhood she definitely didn't miss. As soon as she was old enough to be on her own, she'd made her escape.

Phillip wondered what was going through Lily's head. He could tell that she liked her guest suite. So it had to be something else. But what?

"If you need anything just buzz Edna." He indicated the blue button on the Ivory and gold antique French phone. "Dinner is at six. Or if you're too tired this evening, I can have Edna bring you a tray."

"Will you be dining with us?"

"I'll try to make it home in time. You see I've been covering for a colleague. Hopefully he'll have returned later this afternoon."

"Oh."

Phillip smiled. Did she really want his company? Lily Jordan was full of contradictions. But contradictions he found fascinating. He glanced at his watch.

"I'd better be getting back to the hospital. Relax and enjoy yourself. When you're feeling stronger you can go for a swim."

"Yes, sir." She saluted him.

Phillip grinned. "Did I sound autocratic?"

"Just a little around the edges."

"I guess being a doctor and prescribing for patients all the time makes me that way."

"It means that you care. That's nice."

"A compliment from you, Ms. Jordan?"

"Don't push it, doctor."

"I'd better go while the going is good, he" said heading for the door. "I'll see you later, Lily."

Lily walked into the bedroom and lay down on the bed. She sank her exhausted body into its downy-softness. Her eyes closed and almost immediately she fell asleep.

Phillip found his mother sitting out on the front porch gallery. She had evidently been waiting to talk to him.

"When you were eight, you used to go searching for strays and sneaked them into the house. Is this Lily Jordan another one of your wounded strays?"

"Mother."

"How long will she be staying with us?"

"Two weeks."

"Two weeks!"

"Yes. She's been driving herself way too hard and needs to rest and learn how to relax."

"So you think you're the one to teach her to do this?"

"All right, Mother, what is the point of all this?"

"There's no point—yet."

"But you think there will be in the future?"

"Ms. Jordan is a very attractive young woman and you're a wealthy, handsome doctor."

"Will you ever get beyond outer appearances, Mother, and get to know the inner person. I thought that therapy had cured you of that particular hang-up."

"It's not a hang-up as you put it. I'm concerned about you and—"

"Just don't let it go beyond that. Okay? I choose my own companions."

"You make me sound—"

"Overprotective? Paranoid even? Well?"

"I have been duly put in my place."

"I'll try to get home in time for dinner. Just in case I'm not able to, be nice to Lily," he said softly, but there was steel backing his words.

Phillip sat updating the chart of one of Lawrence Mayfield's patients, the colleague he'd been covering for, when the doctor himself walked into his office. Phillip smiled, relief flooding his mind.

"I can see you're eager to leave. From what I overheard at the nurses' station it's because of a very sexy model named Lily Jordan."

"I should have known the hospital grapevine would move into operation quicker than a speeding bullet. How is your mother, Larry?"

"Oh she's doing fine. She had a mild heart attack. She has to learn her limitations. If I had to pick between her and my father, I'd have thought he'd be the one to have a heart attack."

"Your mother is a busy dedicated doctor, Larry. I wonder where you got your workaholic tendencies?"

"My workaholic tendencies? You should talk. You give new meaning to 24/7, Phil."

He had to laugh. "Guilty as charged."

Larry eyed him thoughtfully. "But this Lily Jordan has made you consider changing all that."

"She's just a patient."

"Not. She's special to you. Admit it. Never mind! Don't. It's about time you became interested in someone and—"

"Joined you in wedded bliss?"

"You're a family man down to your toes and you know it. Is this Lily Jordan in the running?"

"For what?"

"You know what. Oh, Gaby is going to love hearing this."

"Larry. You're not going to tell her, are you? You know how determined your matchmaking wife is to get me married."

"She cares, Phil. She wants to see you happy. And you haven't been since Gina Frazier used your heart for a sidewalk."

"Let's not bring up ancient history."

"It can't be too ancient or you wouldn't still be affected by it."

"I'm not! At least not nearly as much anymore."

Larry grinned. "Glad to hear it. I'd like to meet Ms. Lily Jordan."

"Maybe you will." Phillip glanced at his watch. "If I don't hurry, I won't make it home in time to share dinner with the lady in question."

"By all means don't let me hold you up."

CHAPTER FIVE

Phillip all but raced up the stairs at Magnolia Grove to shower and change. He'd called earlier to make sure that dinner would be served out on the terrace. He didn't want to overwhelm his guest with the austerity of the huge formal dining room. Knowing his mother, she would do it just to make Lily feel uncomfortable. He didn't know what he was going to do about his mother. He wondered if she'd been grilling Lily about her family background. He hoped not.

Just as he made his way out onto the terrace, he saw his mother arranging flowers in a vase.

"Where's Lily?" he asked.

"Edna informed me that she would be here momentarily. You're home early. I don't know how many times I've asked you to surprise me with an early arrival. But would you make the effort? Evidently it takes a woman like Lily Jordan for that to happen."

"Now, Mother, let's not go there. Okay?"

Lily smoothed down the sides of her simple, black slip dress. It was best to be understated with a touch of elegance than over-dressed to the teeth. She didn't want to give her reluctant hostess reason to look down her aristocratic nose at her. Why should she care anyway? The woman was nothing to her.

She's something to him; she's his mother.

With one last look in the mirror Lily left her bedroom through the French doors and headed through the garden to the terrace where the maid Edna had told her dinner would be served. She'd eaten out in sidewalk restaurants and cafes, but knew they wouldn't compare to on-the-terrace dining in a mansion like Magnolia Grove. She didn't know why she was in such awe of this place. It was just a house like any other. Well, maybe not exactly like any other.

"Lily," Phillip called to her, then strode across the terrace to meet her.

She couldn't help smiling. He had made it home in time to share dinner with her. She couldn't explain why it made her feel so pleased, but it did.

Suzette eyed the scene with deliberation. This Lily Jordan was probably used to men fawning over her. Weren't most high fashion models? Most of them had unsavory reputations. Didn't they? She wondered what kind this one had. She would have to find out for herself. Phillip didn't need to know anything about it. She wouldn't give another woman the chance to hurt her son as Gina Frazier had done. That little nobody had the audacity to spurn a Cardoneaux. Suzette had wanted to make her pay, but Phillip refused to let her do anything.

Phillip didn't miss the calculating gleam in his mother's eyes. He would have to have that conversation He had been putting off sooner rather than later. He wouldn't allow her to hurt Lily. He would have thought she had learned her lesson with his brother's wife, Camille. But when it came to being an overprotective mother, she was worse than a paranoid hen with only one chick.

Fifteen minutes later they were all seated at the table eating a fresh Spinach leaf salad appetizer.

"How long have you been modeling, Ms. Jordan?" Suzette asked.

"Since I was eighteen."

"You started young. How old are you now?"

"Mother!"

"It's all right, Phillip." Lily smiled at his mother.

"I'm twenty-eight. I could ask you the same question, but out of respect I won't."

Phillip's mouth twitched. He needn't have worried, Lily could hold her own. He believed that his mother may just have met her match.

After they'd finished dinner, Edna brought out dessert. Flan cake glazed with brandied strawberry sauce.

"I don't think I have room for dessert," Lily groaned.

"I would imagine that models have to watch their weight," Suzette commented.

"Some do, but I never have. I've always been able to eat anything I want and in any quantity. My metabolism seems to burn off the calories almost immediately. Is that the way it is for you? You're very slim, Mrs. Cardoneaux."

Suzette flushed and then cleared her throat. "You said you started modeling at eighteen. What did your family have to say about that?"

Lily's brown eyes darkened to a color as black as tar when she answered. "Nothing."

Phillip watched the transformation that had come over her and knew instinctively that she and her family didn't get along and that was a sore subject.

"Would you like to go for a short walk, Lily?"

"Yes. I'd love to. What I've seen of Magnolia Grove fascinates me. Was it named that because of the many Magnolia trees that grow in perfusion in this part of the state?"

"Actually no. My father told me it was because there weren't any growing on the property or for miles around when my great-great grandfather bought it. He traveled to Martinique and brought back a hundred Magnolia trees. In fact it was there that he met my great-great grandmother, Josette Dupre."

"I'm sure Ms. Jordan isn't interested in the family history, Phillip."

"On the contrary, Mrs. Cardoneaux. I'm fascinated." Lily looked up at Phillip and smiled. "I'm ready to take that walk now, doctor."

"If you will excuse us, Mother."

Lily asked as they strolled down the path. "I'm curious to know if it's just me. Or is it that your mother doesn't like models?"

"I'm the last bird in the nest and she's—"

"Trying to keep you from falling into my wicked clutches."

He laughed. "That's about the size of it. I don't pay any attention to her."

"You don't?"

"I learned a long time ago not to."

"But doesn't it get rather sticky when you bring your lady friends home for dinner?"

"I haven't brought anyone here in a long time."

Lily could tell that there was a story behind that slightly pained expression on Phillip's face and stiff sound in voice. With his looks and wealth it was hard to believe he wasn't married or engaged. Whoever the woman was that hurt him must have deeply wounded the good doctor.

His hand cupping her elbow, Phillip headed for the gazebo.

"What a view!" Lily exclaimed.

"I'm glad there's a full moon so you can take in the spectacular effect its magical glow has on the river." Phillip slipped his arm around Lily's shoulder. He felt her body immediately tense, and then relax. She definitely wasn't immune to him. And he certainly wasn't to her.

"Look, doctor, I'm not looking to get involved. I've been down that road and it was a rough ride."

"Are you unwilling to try it again because you don't like doctors, men or just me in particular?"

"Let's not go there. Okay? It has nothing to do with that. I think we'd better head back to—"

Phillip pulled her into his arms and kissed her. She melted against him after a few moments.

Breathless, she pulled away and said. "I wish you hadn't done that."

"You wanted me to kiss you, Lily."

"I didn't."

"Yes, you did and you're angry with yourself because you enjoyed it."

"If this is why you—"

"Invited you here? No, it isn't. I'll have to admit that the idea is appealing. You're a very beautiful woman and I am attracted to you."

"Well, we can't let it go beyond that."

"Why not? I'm not the guy who hurt you. And don't tell me that all men are alike because you know they're not."

"Let's put it this way, I'm not anxious to get involved with anyone. Period. Okay? So let's go back to the house. If my staying here is going to make it hard for you to—"

"Keep my hands off you? It won't. I invited you here to rest. Anything that happens beyond that between us has to be mutual and evolve naturally. I've never forced myself on an unwilling woman and I don't intend to make you the first."

Lily sensed that she had angered as well as hurt him, and she was sorry for that, but it couldn't be helped. It was the way she felt. No way would she ever open herself up to be hurt by a white man again. When relationships (especially that kind) ended, it hurt too much.

Phillip watched the changing expressions on Lily's face. He wanted to hold her and soothe away all her fears and insecurities. But right now he was sure she wouldn't appreciate it. He was a patient man. And she was, after all, living in his home. Time and proximity was on his side. He would get her to open up to him eventually. He had decided to make Ms. Lily Jordan his special project.

Lily awoke with a start and glanced at the clock on the night stand. It was three o'clock in the morning. What an erotic dream she'd been having about Phillip Cardoneaux. He was walking toward her and for some reason she couldn't move away. When he reached her, he started gently kissing her lips and reverently caressing her breasts through her nightgown. Exciting wonderful sensations strummed through her femininity. Although her head urged her to resist, she was unable to make her body obey. But seeing her golden-brown skin next to his paler lightly tanned one jolted her out of his spell, lending her strength to pull away when he made a move to intimately unite them.

Now as she lay wide awake the image of her mother and father floated before her mind's eye. And the memory of how they had always argued before going into their bedroom and how quiet it instantly became after they closed the door made her shudder. Apparently, there was great sex between them and she was the product of their lust for each other. But beyond that, there was nothing.

It doesn't have to be that way between you and Phillip, the voice of reason intoned. *Relationships are what you make of them.*

Still she feared a relationship with him and vowed she wouldn't have one with him.

If he decides to pursue you, then what are you going to do, girl?

She would just have to find a way to discourage him that's all.

Phillip had watched Lily disappear inside the guest suite. She hadn't looked back. He knew the exact moment when she'd retreated behind that sassy bravado she wore like a second skin. He wondered who had soured her on relationships. Her parents? Or had a white man cruelly used her? The latter possibility angered him. Along with it came frustration because he wanted her in the worst way, but she was his patient. Her well-being had to come first. Once she was well...

He wanted Lily to admit without any pressure or acts of seduction that she wanted him as much as he wanted her.

He knew there wasn't a chance of that happening any time soon. She needed work and time before she reached that point. He would have to woo her slowly or run the risk of scaring her away. Pain was evidently deeply embedded inside this woman and he wanted so badly to heal her. Even though he was a doctor, was he the one to do it? He had started to tell her that he wasn't what he appeared to be. That he was also part black just as she, but he wanted her to want him for the person he was inside, not because of what color he was on the outside. Or from what race she thought he was. Once she could accept him for the person he was then he would tell her. He sensed that he had a monumental task ahead of him but he was convinced that Lily was worth it. There was wildfire passion inside her and he intended to probe as deeply as he had to to bring it to the surface.

CHAPTER SIX

"Lily pad."

"Carey!" Lily exclaimed from the lounge chair she was sitting on by the pool as she sat drying herself after her swim. "I'm glad you came. How did you get past the butler?"

"I didn't actually. When I knocked on the front door and he opened it, his eyebrows must have shot clean off his forehead when he saw me. I told him I was here to see you and he told me you were down by the pool and showed me how to get here. So here I am. How's it going? What does it feel like living in the lap of luxury?"

"It's so peaceful here. I never thought I'd say that about a place and truly enjoy it without being bored."

"Then the doc was right and you really needed the rest. Has he been behaving himself?"

"What do you mean?"

Carey grinned. "You like him, don't you?"

"Of course I do. He's my doctor. What's not to like."

"That wasn't what you thought a few days ago. And you know exactly what I meant. You know what kind of liking I'm talking about. Admit it. You've got the hots for Dr. Phil."

"Carey, please."

"Please what? I see I have competition."

"I'm not the gold cup prize at the end of a race, Carey. I don't feel that way about either one of you."

"You might not about me, but with the good doctor it's a different story." He looked around. "I should go to the car and break out my camera equipment. The scenery around here is a photographer's dream."

"I doubt that Phillip-I mean Dr. Cardoneaux's mother would give you permission."

"She's a snob then? Looking at Dr. Phil, you wouldn't think so."

"He's nothing like her in that way, but he is her son and…"

"I understand. It's been a couple of days since you've been here. You feeling any different?"

"Yes. I'm beginning to relax. It must be the clean fresh country air."

"You think that's all it is?"

"Carey."

"You need me to do anything for you?"

"No, but thanks. There's extra swim wear in the pool house if you want to take a swim."

He grinned. "Don't mind if I do. Maybe if I stick around long enough I'll get to meet the Dragon Lady in the flesh."

Carey had no concept of what he was wishing for. Suzette Cardoneaux would chew him up and spit him out. She didn't tell him that though. She only shook her head and smiled.

Phillip had purposely kept his distance from Lily to give her time and space. The last thing he wanted to do was move too fast. His mother was going to Paris for a week on her annual shopping trip. God is good. And for that he was grateful. He'd planned a picnic for himself and Lily tomorrow. He was elated when Lily agreed to go. With her he never knew from one day to the next how she'd react in any given situation.

That tired haunted look had begun to fade from her lovely face. He couldn't help speculating as to why she had pushed herself to the point of collapse. What drove this fiery, unpredictable woman? For some reason everything about her intrigued him. If he was patient, would she let him close enough to find out what exactly made her tick?

Phillip laughed. Man had been trying to figure out woman from the beginning of time and still didn't have a clue after all these centuries.

Lily's pulse began to beat faster at the sight of Phillip standing in front of her door when she opened it. He was dressed in ordinary blue jeans and a white knit shirt. But it was the way he filled them out that made her insides quiver. His tanned, muscular biceps bulged against his shirt sleeves and the rest of the shirt outlined his magnificent six-pack abs. And those lean athletic thighs and calves encased in his jeans were enough to send a woman's heart into cardiac arrest. She shook her head to clear it. She had to stop doing this. They'd better go on that picnic right now.

She couldn't remember the last time she'd been on one. She'd heard that in the south people moved along at a more leisurely pace, much slower than the city-bred types she was accustomed to. She had seen people having picnics in Central Park in New York in the summertime, but in the city where she had been born and raised, Newark, New Jersey, it was a rare sight.

"Edna and our cook, Mrs. Bradford, prepared the basket. They said to trust them on the menu," Phillip related to Lily as they strolled through the garden and down the path to a secluded knoll overlooking the river, then spread a blanket on the grass.

"It's so beautiful here." She took a deep breath. "I can only imagine what it must have been like to have grown up around such splendor."

"My brother used to tell anyone who would listen that I turned the house into an animal hospital and the grounds into a wildlife preserve because I was always bringing home strays."

"Do you consider me as one of your strays?"

"Would it bother you if I said yes?"

Lily thought for a while. "Not really. The way you treat your patients isn't so bad."

"Any patients?" he asked scooting closer to her on the blanket. "You're not just any patient to me, Lily. You're special."

"Phillip, I—"

"No pressure, only the truth." He shaded his eyes with his hand, then indicated an area in the near distance. "Over there is where my brother and I used to dive off the pier when we were boys."

Lily could tell that Phillip had deep affection and love for his brother. She could almost see the two of them, both probably similar in looks having fun together. And she envied him because she was an only child. But thank heaven her parents hadn't duplicated their mistake by bringing another child into their home to make miserable.

Phillip frowned when the now familiar distant look came into Lily's eyes. She must be delving into the past and comparing it to the here and now and finding it had been seriously lacking. He wanted to ask her questions about that subject, but he hesitated. He didn't want to infringe on her privacy, but he wanted to know everything there was to know about her.

The smell of grass, the feel of warm sunshine on her skin invigorated Lily. It made her feel carefree. She wanted to bury the past and enjoy the present. She would think about the future at a later date.

What exactly does that mean, girl? Is there a possibility that Dr. Phillip Cardoneaux might fit into your world beyond the here and now?

Phillip spread the red, checkerboard table cloth on the blanket, then lifted out a zip lock bag of fried chicken from the picnic basket and took out a drumstick.

"Mrs. Bradford's famous southern-fried chicken is to die for. Try it." He brought it to Lily's lips.

She bit into it. "Hmm, you're right. It's the best I've ever tasted."

"Her special egg potato salad and fresh baked rolls are in here too." He put some of each on her plate and handed it to her, then filled his own.

Phillip lifted out still another container and opened it and grinned.

"My favorite dessert, walnut pineapple cake. I should have guessed. Edna and Mrs. Bradford really know how to pack a picnic basket."

"They evidently do for their favorite person."

Phillip watched the movement of Lily's lips when they closed over her fork as she ate her potato salad. He forced himself to tamp down the desire that ordinary action aroused. He didn't dare let his eyes wander any lower to the yellow shorts and matching top that contrasted so spectacularly with her golden brown skin, giving it a warm, sexy glow. And the way the outfit shaped her curves could drive a man insane. God she was so beautiful, he ached to touch her, make love... He shook the thought away and quickly delved into the basket.

"Ah, a light rose? wine to complement our lunch. Armand our resident winemaker created this special vintage."

"You mean you make your own wine?"

"Only for our own personal use. Probably several dozen cases a year."

Phillip brought out two wine glasses. He filled hers and then his.

"I propose a toast."

"A toast?"

"To your continued improving health."

Lily was awed by what she saw mirrored in his eyes. Something deeper than the obvious fact that he was a dedicated doctor. He didn't give lip service, he was a man of action and compassion. She'd never come across anyone quite like him before. He affected her in ways that confounded her perception of men.

Phillip wondered what he'd said to put that look on her face. Could it be she was seeing him, really seeing him for the first time? He hoped so. She definitely threw him off balance. Was it possible that he had a similar effect on her?

"I didn't see your mother today?"

"She flew to Paris early this morning. She'll be there for at least a week. She's gone on her annual shopping trip. You've probably modeled in some of her favorite haunts."

"Probably. It doesn't bother you that I'm an international model? We are known to live decadent lives."

"Do you? Live a decadent lifestyle, I mean?"

"Not really. When I first started modeling, I did some pretty outrageous things, but I never deliberately set out to hurt anyone. I was just young and wanted to have fun."

"I don't see anything wrong with that. Would you like to go out to dinner with me this evening. I have today and the next two off thanks to Ms. Alice Clayborne. She suggested to the chief of staff that I needed it. And what Alice wants—"

"Alice gets. She's very fond of you, you know."

"Yes, I know." He cleared his throat. "About my dinner invitation." He tensed inwardly as he waited for her answer.

"I'd like that."

"I'll come by the guest suite at seven."

Lily gasped when she saw his eyes deepen to an exciting smoldering shade of blue, and his lips slip into a devastatingly sexy smile. Her stomach fluttered and her heart beat a little faster and her body heated.

Whoa, girl, you'd better watch yourself around this man. He's most definitely dangerous to your emotional equilibrium. Just how do you propose to resist him?

She didn't have an answer for that question.

CHAPTER SEVEN

Lily searched through her closet for something to wear for her dinner date with Phillip. Nothing seemed right. She called Christine and asked her to bring a few more of her things from her hotel apartment. She explained what she wanted for the evening.

"It must be a pretty special date, huh?" Christine asked as she helped Lily spread out the array of evening dresses she'd brought.

"No. Just a dinner date."

"You sure it's not more than that? I haven't seen you this concerned about what to wear on just a simple dinner date. Is the date with your doctor?"

"I see Carey has been gossiping again. Why do you ask?"

"Carey said you were interested in him more as a man than as a doctor."

"I'm going to kill him."

Christine laughed. "So it's true. I'd say it was about time you got interested in another man after—"

"Don't mention his name! He's a part of the past I don't ever want to think about."

"But, Lily—"

"I mean it Chris." Lily eased her lips into a smile, reaching for a change of subject because Kenton Davies wasn't one she ever intended to discuss with anyone. "I know you're crazy about Carey, so why haven't you let him know?"

"He doesn't even know I'm alive. I'm dull as dish water compared to you."

"No, you're not. Carey doesn't really want me, he just thinks he does. It's more of an ego trip on his part. He knows that I don't care about him like that and never will. So, my dear, you have the field all to yourself."

Lily picked up a rose colored slip dress with creamy lace straps.

"What do you think?"

"It's nice, but the red one is really hot. And you'll look fabulous in it. But then you look fabulous in anything you wear."

"That kind of attitude is not going to fly, my dear Christine. We're going to have to work on your self-esteem. If you got it flaunt it as the old saying goes. Girl, you have a good figure and beautiful hair."

"Thanks. Don't worry I won't turn down any help or advice you can give me if it will get a certain photographer to take notice," she said wistfully.

"If it isn't our own Dr. Phil," Camille quipped when she opened the door to her brother-in-law.

Phillip kissed her on the cheek. "Where are the two demons you and Nicholas keep trying to convince me are my niece and nephew?"

"They're in the family room playing with their father. What brings you to our neck of the woods? Not that you need a reason."

"You know there is one. You're very perceptive, Camille."

"This reason wouldn't have anything to do with a certain house-guest staying at Magnolia Grove. Would it?"

Phillip shook his head. "I might have known you'd heard about that."

"Your mother mentioned it to Nicholas." Camille monitored his reaction. "She hasn't been—"

"Interfering? No. Not yet."

"But you expect her to and you're worried about it. Aren't you?"

"It's not so much that. It's just that Lily is—I don't know how to describe her."

Camille smiled. "Hallelujah! You've finally taken an interest in somebody other than Gina Frazier. I told you that in time you would forget the woman's name."

"Yes, you did. Camille, Lily's so different. I've never met anyone like her."

"If you want her, then use some of the Cardoneaux charm on her. It worked on me."

"What worked on you?" Nicholas said entering the room with Xavier and Solange, one squirming toddler tucked under each arm.

Camille took Solange and kissed her fat little café-au-lait colored cheek. "I was telling Phillip how effectively the Cardoneaux charm worked."

Nicholas kissed his wife's lips. "Worked?"

"Still is working, baby."

"All right you two." Phillip laughed. "You're an old married couple."

"That may be true, but what we have just keeps getting better and better, little brother."

"Yes, indeed it does," Camille seconded with a smile.

"So you came to learn the secret to our success?" Nicholas asked.

Camille looked from one brother to the other. "It's nap time for the children. I'll leave you two to discuss strategy." She laughed, leading Xavier and Solange from the living room.

"You have a rare gem in Camille, Nick."

"I know. So how can I help my favorite brother?"

"Only brother. As you no doubt heard from our mother, we have a houseguest. Well, she's not your ordinary houseguest."

"She's beautiful and you're attracted to her. And after that fiasco with Gina Frazier, you're uncertain how to proceed. Right?"

"Yeah."

"I could ring Gina Frazier's neck for what she did to you."

"She's the past and I'm hoping Lily will be a part of my future."

"Oh, so it's like that. I remember thinking that after meeting Camille. Our situation was so complicated and I didn't know from one day to the next how it was going to turn out. But love won out in the end. Are you saying you're in love with this Lily Jordan?"

"I don't know the answer to that yet. I want her and like being with her."

"Tell me about her."

"As you know, she's my patient and a houseguest at Magnolia Grove. She's also an international Supermodel. There's something wild, and I don't know, earthy and carefree about her."

"It's more than her obvious beauty that interests you though isn't it?"

"Yes. She's gutsy and a little prickly."

"Kind of like a cactus lily. I remember when I met Camille, I likened her to a strong flower. Is it our fate to be drawn to such women? I wonder."

"What advice can you give me, Nick?"

"Where the heart is concerned, you can't always predict the outcome."

"You mean I'm on my own."

"Pretty much. I can tell you this, don't be a fool and rush in blindly. Take your time and really get to know this woman."

"I certainly didn't do that with my last relationship.

Did I?"

"We all make mistakes. I never thought Gina Frazier was good enough for you. She loved going out and partying and having you spend huge sums of money on her. She got her wish for a big spender when she married Gerald Cannon. He's wealthy and loves indulging his women. But I have to wonder if she's really happy. I know Gerry, and although he may be generous to a fault, he's possessive in the extreme. If the new Mrs. Cannon had any ideas about spreading herself around, she knows better now, I'll bet."

Phillip cleared his throat. "Getting back to Lily. I'm taking her out to dinner this evening. I've reserved a private dining room at Gautreau's. The trouble is how am I going to keep my hands off her. She's sexy as hell, man. I don't want to rush things, but she's temptation on a pair of long shapely legs."

"She must be something for you to consider giving in to it. I'd like to meet her."

"You sound like Larry. I'll have to throw a party and introduce her to everyone."

"You'll have to bring her over to meet us before that. When you decide on a date for the party let us know. Camille wouldn't want to miss it. She's been concerned about you for a while."

"I know. Well, I'd better go. Would Sunday be a good day to bring Lily over?"

"I'll have to check with Camille, but as far as I know it would be all right. I'll have to get back to you about it."

As Nicholas watched Phillip leave, he hoped his brother had found the right woman this time. His ex-fiancée had put him through hell.

CHAPTER EIGHT

It was almost seven. Lily took one last look in the full-length cheval mirror. She didn't know why she felt so nervous. She was just having dinner with Phillip. That didn't mean...

What? Admit it, you're looking forward to more?

She wasn't. She had absolutely no aspirations in that direction.

Who are you trying to convince?

Lily heard a knock at the door. She smoothed her hands down the sides of her dress and went to answer it. When she opened the door Phillip was standing there looking like a woman's most wicked fantasy. His black curly hair gleamed like a glossy raven's wing under the soft hall chandelier light. Dinner jackets were created to emphasize just such a perfect body as Phillip Cardoneaux possessed. She'd seen and worked with male models who didn't come close to looking as good in his clothes as this man. That killer grin of his made the bottom of her stomach drop to her knees.

"You ready to come with me, pretty lady?"

Anywhere you chose to take me. Where did that come from? What was the matter with her?

"Where are we going?"

"Let it be surprise."

"I take it we won't be dining at Mickey D's?"

Phillip laughed. "Not hardly. You'll enjoy the place I'm taking you. I promise."

Lily had heard of Gautreau's, but hadn't dined there. It was renowned for it's excellent international cuisine. The intimate ambiance drew you in the moment you entered the restaurant.

Phillip observed her reaction sensing that she was pleased. It had been a long time since he'd taken care to see that his companion felt that way. Not since Gina Frazier. And that said a lot about the affect Ms. Lily Jordan had on him.

The maitre d' directed them to a private dining room up the elegant spiral staircase.

Lily's eyes widened in delight. She hadn't expected this. The only thing wrong was that being so private with

Phillip would undoubtedly cause tension between them; tension of the sensual variety. As one of the nurses at the hospital had commented, he was one gorgeous hunk of man. And very masculine and very sexy. But he was much more than even that. He was strong, compassionate and a dedicated healer. She sensed that he was trying to heal her in more ways than simply the physical. He just didn't know that there was nothing he could do about the emotional side of her. That was off limits. She'd never let him or any man get that close to her again.

The waiter handed them menus and asked. "May I recommend the Caneton Roti, roast duckling?"

"That sounds wonderful," Lily commented looking over the menu to see what came with it. Could you create a prawn salad with spinach leaves and artichokes. And I'd like the olive oil and lemon pepper salad dressing."

"I'll have the same, but with spicy tomato french dressing."

"The wine steward will join you momentarily, sir and madam," he said taking their menus and leaving them alone.

Lily rose from her chair and walked over to the window and looked out. "This uptown location is breathtaking. You get to witness the sun gilding the buildings as it sets. The effect is almost magical."

Phillip joined her. "It is pretty impressive, isn't it?"

"New Orleans is an impressive, exhilarating city. I'm sorry I missed the Mardi Gras."

"It can get crazy during that season. I prefer late spring and late summer. Although the humidity can become oppressive at times."

"You haven't experienced oppressive humidity until you've spent time in New Jersey during late summer. And also Memphis and Portugal."

"Then New Orleans is probably nothing compared to the many

places you've traveled in your experiences as an international model."

"I wouldn't say that. I've never seen so many different varieties of things as I have here in New Orleans."

"As exhausted as you were when you were admitted to the hospital, I would have thought that you hadn't found the time to make that discovery."

"The first two weeks we were here, there had been a few obstacles in our shooting schedule, like the early morning rains, and the humidity which nearly drove the hairdressers crazy because they had to repeatedly redo the models' hairdos. And some of the designs we modeled didn't stand up well under those conditions, so I got to do a little sightseeing especially around the wharf."

"So you tried to make up for lost time by working yourself into the ground."

"Phillip."

"That's just a true observation. After talking to Mimi at the agency, she said she'd never made it mandatory that you do that. She added that you've always been a workaholic and even she didn't have a clue as to what drives you."

"Is there something wrong with wanting a successful career and doing everything you can to make it happen?"

"No, not if you put things in their proper perspective."

"Meaning?"

"Meaning you should put your health first."

"You're a doctor. Quite naturally you'd take that stand," she inserted.

"So are we back to square one? Please, can we call a truce? I want to enjoy the rest of the evening."

"I'm sorry, I never meant to—you just seem to bring out all my defensive mechanisms."

"I don't mean to."

"Truce sounds good. Our dinner has arrived."

Phillip watched Lily tuck into her food. There was nothing wrong with her appetite now. He was glad to see it. Was he making progress with her by having her recuperate at Magnolia Grove? Maybe physically, but she'd erected barriers to guard her emotional responses. What could he do to tear them down and reach the real Lily Jordan.

Lily wondered what was going through Phillip's mind as he watched her. The desire she'd seen shining in his eyes when she opened the guest suite door earlier that evening was unmistakable. But he hadn't acted on it. Most men she'd met wouldn't have shown that degree of self-control. Phillip Cardoneaux seemed to be the exception to the rule. He'd kissed her, but he hadn't pushed things any farther than she had allowed him to.

"I've had a wonderful evening, Phillip."

"You seem surprised. Why is that?"

"I can't explain it really. You confuse me, doctor."

"In what way?"

"Like I said, I can't explain it."

"Do you have to have an explanation for everything, Lily?"

"Of course I do. It's the only way to know how to react in any given situation."

"Can't you just go with the flow?"

"I've been there, done that with disastrous results. And I don't intend to travel that path again."

"It doesn't necessarily have to end in disaster if we leave the old baggage behind and start out fresh as if the past had never happened."

"It's easier said than done."

"True, but we have to try."

"You're an eternal optimist."

"It's funny you should say that. My mother calls me that too. And the two of you are as alike as chalk and cheese."

"Which one am I? I'm afraid to find out the answer."

Phillip grinned. "I love your sense of humor."

"Can we take a walk down by the river before we turn in?"

"You think you'll be safe from me if we do that?"

"Phillip."

"I like the idea of taking a moonlight stroll with you."

Lily wondered if it was such a good idea considering the attraction between them.

Girl nothing you do is going to change that. Be honest you know you wouldn't want it to.

Phillip smiled. He knew how hard Lily was fighting the chemistry brewing between them. But the question was why? Was it fear of failing in a relationship that worried her so much? If that were the case he knew the feeling only too well. Maybe they could help each other heal their emotional wounds.

Over the last few days Lily had enjoyed Magnolia Grove's tranquil beauty. It was definitely the ideal place to recharge one's batteries. She glanced at Phillip. It didn't hurt having gorgeous human scenery to add to your appreciation, she thought as she and Phillip strolled down the road paralleling the Mississippi leading to the family's private pier. It was like a small kingdom here. Such grandeur was only to be imagined, but here she was a guest of the Cardoneauxs.

"What is going through that lovely head of yours, Lily?"

"I'm still trying to understand why you invited me here?"

"It was the only place I could think of where I knew with certainty you'd get some rest."

"But this is your home."

"Yes. It is. I want you to know that I did it because you're special to me, Lily. Don't ask me why I feel that way about you because I can't answer your question. All I know is that I wanted you here."

"But that doesn't make sense unless–no that can't be it because you've been a complete gentleman."

"That's not quite true. I wasn't able to stop myself from kissing you. And right now I want to do it again."

"As long as you understand that it can't go beyond that."

"Why can't it?"

"Because I won't allow it. I'm getting tired and I think we'd better head back to the house."

"Why do you keep running from me, Lily?"

"I'm not doing that"

"I'm not going to hurt you."

"I believe you wouldn't intentionally. It's just that I don't want to get involved."

"Since you know I won't hurt you, what are you afraid of?"

"I'm not afraid of anything. Oh, God, Phillip. Don't do this to me."

He pulled her into his arms. "I will never do anything you don't want me to."

"The problem is I want you to do a lot of things to me, but I can't let it happen. I won't."

"You've been pretty badly hurt. Haven't you?" He'd like to strangle the man who'd done this to her. He may not have been physically abusive, but whatever he'd done had amounted to the same thing. With similar but more far-reaching results. The bastard had completely shattered her trust.

Phillip remembered, when he'd done his six months internship in the psych ward of the state hospital, the emotional wreckage resulting from unforgivable treatment done by one human being to another had turned his stomach. He empathized with the patients to such a profound degree that he'd almost decided to specialize in psychiatry.

He recognized that same pain in Lily. He realized that he was going to have to be careful with her and move slowly. It didn't matter how long it might take, he had no intention of giving up on her. She was as attracted to him as he was to her. That had to count for something. At least it was a start.

"It looks like it's going to rain. We should head back. I don't want you caught in a downpour."

Lily hadn't expected him to let the conversational ball drop there. Other men she'd known wouldn't have. But then Phillip Cardoneaux was not like any other man she'd ever met. There was a gentleness and decency about him that was completely disarming. And of course there was his sex appeal. Not to mention his magnificent body.

Just as they reached the front gallery of the house, the rain started coming down. The smell of warm moist earth and lush greenery floated up their nostrils as the rain soaked the grounds.

Phillip and Lily stood silently watching nature in action for a few minutes.

Lily yawned. "I'm sorry, but I really am tired."

"The pungent, rain-washed scent in the air does tend to make you drowsy. It has never failed to do that to me. I can understand why my great-great grandfather fell in love with Magnolia Grove."

"So can I."

"You can? Does that communion of minds make us soulmates?"

"I guess in a way it does." She smiled. Phillip Cardoneaux was nothing short of charmingly irresistible. Which also made him dangerous. That thought sobered her. "Whatever way works, I'll take it," he said, then taking her hand, led her into the house.

When they reached the guest wing, Phillip opened the door and turned to Lily. The play of the ceiling lights on her hair brought out the blond-gold highlights, forming a halo around her head.

"Why are you looking at me like that?" she asked.

"Because you are absolutely beautiful."

So was he, she thought. It was going to be hell keeping herself in check around him. He was a temptation she didn't know how long she could resist if he continued to pursue her. No matter the length of her stay at Magnolia Grove, recuperation while being in such close proximity to Phillip was going to seem like a year of torture.

He kissed away the frown of uneasiness between her velvety brown brows. "Let each day take care of itself, Lily."

That was what she did not dare to do because it could lead them to a place where they could not go.

You can go there, girl, but you are just too afraid.

No. She wasn't.

"Lily, are you all right?"

"Yes," she answered absently."

"You don't have to worry, I won't bore you any longer with my company."

"Phillip, please don't be angry with me."

"I'm not angry, Lily. I'll say good night."

As she watched him leave something inside urged her to call him back, but she battled it into submission. She had to be strong. Her emotional well being depended on it. She hadn't meant to hurt Phillip, but knew she had judging from the look on his face when he walked away.

What could she do? She'd agreed to recuperate at Magnolia Grove and she was just barely a week into the bargain. It was a relief that his mother was out of the country. Something about Lily rubbed the older woman the wrong way. Or was it that she was just being overprotective of her son?

Phillip wasn't the kind of man who would let his mother dictate his life. But Suzette Cardoneaux was no ordinary mother. She was like a tigress protecting her one and only cub. Which meant that any woman in his life had better be prepared to do battle with her. Why was she even thinking about that? There was no way she was going to get involved with Phillip in a personal way. So his mother had nothing to worry about from her.

You are really something Lily Jordan. For one thing you're a coward.
No, she wasn't.
Yes, you are. You're afraid to fight for what you want because you haven't got the guts to rise above the past and reach for the future.
She refused to dwell on what could never be.

Coward, coward echoed through her mind. She ran into the bathroom and turned on the shower to drown out the reverberations. But it didn't do any good. As she finished her shower and dried herself, she could still hear that word and knew her conscience spoke the truth.

Phillip paced the confines of the balcony outside his bedroom. Lily Jordan was making him crazy. He'd promised himself that he would woo her slowly, really give himself time to get to know her, but it was harder than he ever imagined it to be. She was fighting herself more than she was fighting him. How was he ever going to reach her? His mother would be back next week and he would have to go back to the hospital. Time wasn't exactly on his side any more. Lily would be leaving in another week.

He smiled. He wondered if she knew how to ride. They could go riding tomorrow afternoon. But what if she didn't ride? Then he'd have the pleasure of teaching her. He could show her the small winery. Or he could show her the neighboring mansions and estates.

The key was to stay in close proximity to his house guest. Not too close, but just close enough. He would call Larry and arrange to have two more days off. After all he owed him a favor.

In your face Lily Jordan is where I intend to be for the next few days. I'll break down those walls you've built around yourself. With that he walked back into his bedroom.

CHAPTER NINE

Phillip glanced at his watch as he waited for Lily to make an appearance at breakfast. He'd all but given up when she walked in.

"Good morning," she said with a smile. "Sorry I'm late. I kind of overslept."

"It's all right. You're here for that express purpose. Do you ride?"

"You mean horses? As a matter of fact, I do, but it's been a long time. I learned how on my first photo shoot. It was the designer's premiere riding gear line and he insisted that the model look as though she was an expert. At the time I was afraid of horses." She laughed. "I tried to get out of doing the shoot, but the designer was adamant that I be the one to model his clothes. He said I had a healthy outdoors look about me."

"Well, I'm glad you know how. Would you like to go for a ride this afternoon?"

What could she say? Without his company she knew she'd be bored and to her, boredom was the kiss of death.

"I don't have a riding outfit."

"Not a problem. I have a cousin that is about your size and she left her riding gear the last time she came for a visit. So it's a go for this afternoon?"

"Yes."

"I'll have Edna bring the outfit to you at twelve."

He had an answer for everything, she thought shaking her head.

Phillip saw the amused expression on Lily's face. He could hear the walls rumble. They were definitely weakening. "How about a quick swim. It's unusually warm this morning."

'I'll meet you at the pool in fifteen minutes," Lily answered.

Phillip swallowed hard when Lily appeared at the pool. What she did for a bikini was a heart attack waiting to happen. Eat your heart out Halle Berry. Lily's pert rounded breasts filled the top to almost, but not quite overflowing. He could span her tiny waist with his two hands. And the thought of sliding his fingers over her softly rounding hips and butt...

Phillip stood up as she approached.

Lily grinned. The good doctor was speechless. She knew she looked good in her apricot bikini. She reveled in the appreciation she saw in his eyes. A lot of men looked at her that way, but when Phillip did it, she felt special.

His athletic build definitely turned her on.

"How do you keep so fit, doctor?"

"Swimming, riding and I work out once a week at my health club." He smiled. "I take it you like the results?"

"Yes, indeed I do."

"You can have an up close and personal inspection any time," he said drawing her into his arms.

"I thought you invited me for a swim, doctor."

"So I did."

A mischievous twinkle came into Phillip's eyes.

"Oh no! Phillip, you wouldn't?" She slipped out of his embrace and made a run for it.

He caught her easily and leaped into the water with her in his arms, then let her go and swam away laughing.

Lily went under and came up sputtering. "I'm going to get you for that," she said and started after him.

Phillip purposely eluded her for a few minutes, then stopped and allowed her to catch up with him. She stopped a few feet in front of him, then dove beneath the surface and came up under Phillip knocking his legs out from under him, dumping him in the water.

When he came up for air, Lily was a few feet away grinning like a Cheshire cat. The sound of her laughter was so contagious Phillip had to laugh too.

Lily felt invigorated. She hadn't had this much fun in a long time. It was amazing how doing silly stuff could perk you up.

He's what you need in your life, girl.

The feeling faded. She didn't need anybody, especially not a white man.

Phillip picked up on the change in her. Whatever happened in the past was evidently deep-seated and from time to time resurfaced. He climbed out of the pool and picked up a towel and waited for Lily to get out and handed her one. They walked over to the lounge chairs where Edna had left a pitcher of orange juice and two glasses on the table beneath the huge umbrella.

"When is your mother due back?" Lily asked.

"Next Friday. Don't tell me you've missed her?"

"Believe it or not I have. She keeps people on their toes."

"And she is the perfect buffer between the two of us.

You don't need her for that. As I said before, I won't do anything you don't want me to do."

Phillip rose from the lounge chair. "I'll meet you at the stable at one o'clock."

Lily had to admit that the riding outfit the maid had brought to her fit as though it had been made for her. It was even in her favorite buff and chocolate brown colors.

She was experiencing such conflicting emotions where Phillip was concerned. She knew there could never be anything between them and yet she craved his touch, the sound of his voice, the feel of his lips on hers.

Phillip was waiting in the stable for Lily. He had on a blue plaid shirt, riding jeans and black boots. He was evidently a serious rider, no polo-playing aristocrat.

Phillip smiled. His cousin never looked that good in the riding outfit.

"Are you ready to go?"

"Any time you are, doctor."

They rode past several historical mansions and Phillip gave her a shortened down summary of their history.

"I hope I'm not boring you."

"Oh, you're not. My father's family owned a plantation similar to these. Unfortunately it was sold shortly after the Korean War. Since coming to stay at Magnolia Grove, I've wondered what it would have been like to see Grand Oaks at the peak of his magnificence. I learned that it has been turned into a bed and breakfast."

Since Magnolia Grove was such an integral part of his heritage Phillip wondered what it would be like to lose it. Or not be close to his family. Family was important to him. He hated seeing his brother move out of Magnolia Grove, but he understood and respected his reasons for doing so. If it came down to living there or losing his family, he also would have moved out.

He wanted a happy marriage like his brother had with Camille, and he was beginning to feel more and more that Lily was the one who could give him that. He could picture a little girl with her dark exotic eyes and golden-brown skin. He was getting ahead of himself. First he had to make the stubborn woman realize how much he cared for her and that no matter what the problems were, they could solve them together if she would just learn to trust him.

Because you feel that way about her doesn't necessarily follow that she'll fall in love with you.

He was going to do everything in his power to make it impossible for her not to.

Phillip asked. "Would you like to visit our winery?"

"Yes, I would."

As they rode back to Magnolia Grove, they passed pastures with thoroughbred horses and fat cattle grazing contentedly on the thick grass, completely oblivious to them. They came to a stream that divided Cardoneaux property from their nearest neighbor's and stopped to let the horses drink.

"Magnolia Grove had been reduced from five thousand acres to fifty when my father sold the land to start Cardoneaux Construction. After my brother made a success of the architectural addition to the business, he bought back a hundred and fifty acres. We turned fifty of it into a vineyard and fifty into a fruit orchard. The rest is used for our horses.

"Sounds like a fairytale existence."

"Not always. We've had problems like everyone else."

"The tart smell of grapes is so intoxicating."

"Would you like to sample the wine we make from them?"

"Maybe just one glass. It usually goes to my head if I drink more than that. I've learned that I'm the world's cheapest drunk."

Phillip laughed as they headed toward the winery.

"It's good you have come to taste this year's vintage, monsieur." Armand greeted Phillip and smiled.

"He only acts subservient in front of company," Phillip quipped. "Armand, Lily Jordan. She's a guest at the house."

"You are very beautiful, Miss Jordan."

"Thank you for saying that. But please just call me Lily. May I call you Armand?"

"I'd like that very much. I've been experimenting with apples and grapes and have come up with a refreshing wine. Would you like to taste it, Lily?"

"Oh, yes."

Phillip watched Lily interact with Armand. She displayed no sign of snobbery. In fact she treated everyone the same, even his mother. When he thought about his mother and how she never failed to put the servants and workers in their place... In hindsight he remembered that Gina was also a snob. That was one thing about her that he had disliked.

He noticed how Lily took tiny sips from each wine. He was sure that she wasn't aware that what she drank amounted to more than one glass. Her cheeks were flushed and her reserved manner soon disappeared.

When Armand left to attend to a problem with one of the workers, Lily started talking.

"You know, Phillip, I envy you growing up at Magnolia Grove. I think I'm a country girl at heart, but alas I was raised in the city."

"I'd say for a city girl you turned out all right."

"You really think so? Well," she said swirling her wine in the glass, "let me tell you, my parents spent so much time going at each other, that in the meantime I practically raised myself. You know they used to even argue about where I got my nose, from her family or his. I used to lock myself in my room and turn up the sound on the TV. When I think about it, the only time they weren't arguing or bickering was when they closed their bedroom door. And then, and only then was there ever any peace in the house.

Phillip took the glass from Lily. "I think we should be getting back to the house." And escorted her out of the building.

"I didn't mean to say all those things in there. You're just so easy to talk to."

Phillip smiled. She actually opened up to him. It was just a crack, but he was actually making progress.

Back in her room Lily opened the French doors and looked out over the garden. She still couldn't believe what she'd told Phillip. She'd never discussed herself or her family with anyone, not even Carey. But with Phillip she had turned into a CD player permanently stuck on play. She didn't know what had come over her.

God she was tired. She headed for the bathroom to take a shower. Feeling refreshed afterward, she slipped between the sheets and fell asleep.

When she woke up, she felt rested and a little embarrassed by her behavior earlier. She got out of bed and walked over to the closet and pulled out a short white sun dress with straps that crisscrossed in back. She chose white strappy high heel sandals and slipped her feet into them. She was tall. But even though she would be wearing heels, she knew Phillip would be taller than she.

Lily was impressed when she and Phillip walked out on the terrace. The table was set for two with elegant bone china, crystal stem ware and a single yellow rose placed in a delicately sculptured crystal vase adorned the center of the table. The setting was most definitely romantic.

Phillip walked around the French lace-covered table and pulled out a chair for Lily. As she lowered herself into it, he stood behind her chair. The scent of his cologne wrapped around her senses and she quivered with awareness. He had to know what he was doing to her. He was making it next to impossible for her to resist the pull of attraction.

She breathed a sigh of relief when Edna arrived with a food trolley and uncovered their meal. Lily remembered mentioning to Phillip that she liked seafood. He'd evidently had the cook prepare her favorite, Lobster steamed in wine with herb Sauce. There was also a dish of buttered Artichoke Hearts. And for dessert Orange Mousse.

As soon as the maid had left, Lily took a keen interest in her food not daring to look Phillip in the eye.

He was aware of her attempt to appear aloof and he smiled.

"The dinner is fabulous, Phillip. It's the best Lobster and artichokes I've eaten in a while. I'll have to make a point of complimenting Mrs. Bradford."

"She's an excellent cook, but my friend, Jolie, who happens to be a chef at Antoine's, makes the most incredible, out-of-this-world peanut butter pie you will ever eat. It literally melts in your mouth."

Lily wondered if this Jolie was more than a friend and in actuality the woman who had hurt Phillip. When she had asked him about his past earlier she could tell that it pained him to talk about it. But now he acted as though they were still friends.

Seeing her confusion Phillip said, "Jolie's husband owns an art gallery and they live above the shop on Conti in the French Quarter."

"What kind of paintings does he display?"

"A variety. He displays a few of my brother's works from time to time."

Lily frowned. "I thought you told me that he was an architect and ran the family business?"

"I did and he does, but he is also an artiste."

She smiled. "I can see that you are very proud of him."

"We can go to the gallery tomorrow. I believe Henri is currently displaying a few of Nicholas's paintings. At the same time you can meet Jolie and sample her cooking for yourself. I've known her and Henri for years. In fact my brother and I and Henri used to play together when we were little boys."

Phillip waited for her reaction. When there wasn't one, he thought about it. She had evidently assumed that Jolie and Henri were white. He wondered what she would think when she met them.

"I'd love to go."

"Good. Afternoon is the best time to go to the gallery. Their two children will be visiting with their maternal grandparents."

So she wasn't the one after all. Lily wondered if she would ever meet the woman who had hurt Phillip. What difference did it make? It wasn't as though she harbored any hope of having a permanent relationship with him. As far as she was concerned it was a moot point. But she knew the possibility of her escaping without at least a bruised heart was slim to none.

Phillip picked up on the sudden change in Lily and had an idea what caused it. The walls of her reserve were going up again.

"Lily, would you like to go into New Orleans and make the rounds of nightclubs. I know it can get boring out here and I know you're used to a different and faster pace of living."

"Not tonight, Phillip, I think I'll just turn in early." As she started to rise from her chair, he was around the table helping her before she could stand.

Lily's heart beat quickened at his nearness and she closed her eyes, silently praying to get through the next few minutes without succumbing to his seductive charm.

"It's only 7:30. Take a walk with me, Lily. We seem to be turning it into a ritual."

She sighed. A part of her wanted to say yes, but another part urged her to run as fast as she could as far as she could.

"I'll walk you back to your suite." Phillip cupped her elbow and guided her through the central garden, along the path leading to the much smaller garden and terrace. When they reached the French doors, he opened them.

"I'll be ready to leave for the gallery at noon. Good night, Phillip."

As Lily moved to go inside the room, Phillip grasped her arm and turned her around and kissed her deeply.

That kiss set her soul on fire making her crave for more.

"Oh, tiger Lily, you drive me out of my mind with wanting you," he murmured in her ear and picked her up and carried her inside and lowered her onto the lounging couch by the door, then sat down beside her.

"Phillip, I don't think—" she moaned as she felt his hand slide down her back and caress, then gently squeeze her buttocks.

"Tell me you don't want me as much as I want you and I'll stop."

Her mind urged her to say the words, but she couldn't because it wasn't true. She did want him. God, how she wanted him. When he unfastened the straps at the back of her dress, she gasped. His warm fingers caressing her bare skin made her tremble with desire. When those same fingers found her breast and stroked the nipple, she nearly melted in her shoes.

"Let me make love to you, my tiger Lily." He lowered the bodice of her sundress and brushed his tongue across one nipple, then played equal attention to the other. When he returned to the first one, he covered it with his mouth and sucked strongly. Her moan of pleasure spurred him on.

"Phillip, oh, Phillip, I–"

He left her breast and stopped the flow of her words with his lips melding on hers.

A few seconds later, he eased his lips away and said, "I know you want me, Lily. Stop fighting it, sweetheart."

Lily felt as if she were drowning in ecstasy. It was like slowly sinking in the quicksand of rapture. The sensually charged sounds in her voice and Phillip's penetrated the fog she had been drifting in, and suddenly it wasn't her and Phillip's voices, but that of her parents groaning in pleasure as they satisfied their lust for each other. It was enough to completely douse the fire that had blazed to life inside her.

"We–I can't do this, Phillip."

"Don't tell me to stop now, Lily."

She pushed out of his arms and eased the bodice up over breasts and stood up. "Please go–maybe I should leave Magnolia Grove."

"Lily, what happened." He rose from the lounge. "You were with me all the way just now, then suddenly..."

"I'm sorry. Believe me, I wasn't trying to lead you on. Please, just go."

Phillip took a deep breath and mentally forced his arousal to subside. Then he backed away from Lily.

"I'll see you in the morning at breakfast."

"Phillip, please don't be angry with me."

"I'm not angry."

"Maybe I should have breakfast in my room."

"No. I want you to join me. If you don't I'll come get you. Good night, Lily."

How many near disasters could she avert, she thought, as she watched Phillip stride through the garden. Why did he have to be so fine and so darned sexy?

That's not the reason you're trying so hard to avoid getting involved with him. It's what you are beginning to feel for him that's the real problem. He's not Kenton Davies. You don't have to fight your feelings for Phillip. He's the real deal, girlfriend. Let him love you.

Is there any guarantee that I won't get hurt? Her conscience was conspicuously silent. She knew that with love there was none. What was she going to do?

"Don't even think about leaving, Lily. I'll find you and bring you back."

She hadn't realized that he had returned.

"Phillip. It might be for the best."

"No, it wouldn't." He stepped closer and closer still to Lily until they were barely a breath away from touching. "I'm going to get past your damned defenses and make you face the truth. And when I do there will be no stopping me. I'm going to make you mine in more than the Biblical sense, Lily Jordan." He cupped her face in his two hands and kissed her lips, then again more deeply until she was trembling. "I want you to remember that kiss and me and how we affect each other."

As she watched him leave again, Lily raised her fingers to her tender lips. That last kiss said she already belonged to him. It terrified her because deep down she knew it was the truth. No matter what happened in the future she'd be forever haunted by it and him.

CHAPTER TEN

Phillip phoned the hospital to get a report on his patients early Saturday morning. Strangely enough there had been no emergencies or any urgent need to come in. It was as if fate were conspiring to help him get the woman he loved. Yes, he loved her. He'd learned more about himself since knowing her than he had ever known before. He desired her with a desperation that really shook him. She was beautiful, sassy and prickly as hell, but he loved her and wanted her, warts and all. What now? He could sense that she was trying to escape what she was beginning to feel for him.

His behavior last night was so unlike him. He'd felt like the proverbial Neanderthal, complete with primitive longings, savage possessiveness and territorial mentality to go with it. He couldn't let her leave. He didn't want to live his life without her. That in itself surprised him because he'd never felt that way about Gina or any other woman.

He realized he should have told Lily about his dual heritage, but he was sure she would have used the fact that he'd kept it from her as an excuse to defuse what was happening between them. And that he would not do. He hoped that Jolie could help him. If Lily spoke to someone who could sympathize and actually knew how she felt she would come away with a different outlook about her parents. And a deeper understanding about herself and her conflicting emotions where he was concerned.

Phillip was drinking his coffee when Lily walked out onto the terrace. He put the cup down and then stepped around the table and pulled out a chair for her. He was instantly chilled by her cool reserved manner.

"Lily, I want you to know that I–"

"Don't go there, Phillip, not now , not today. All right?"

"Not talking about it won't change what is happening between us.

It won't change the way we feel about each other. Whether you choose to acknowledge it or not."

Lily was silent for a moment, then she lifted the lid from the serving tray and helped herself to scrambled eggs and bacon.

"You are really something, Lily Jordan. You're the stubbornest, most strong-willed woman I have ever met."

"And what about you? You're determined to make things happen between us despite my feelings on the subject. I can't and won't get involved with you."

"You're already involved, Lily. From the first day we met we've been involved with each other. I have never pursued a woman the way I have you. I've never felt for any woman what I feel for you. You bring out in me something so completely foreign it blows me away."

"Well, we'll both just have to get over it."

"I could sooner stop breathing. Don't you understand, woman. You're in my blood as I am in yours. Accept it and we can go on from there. I know it happened really fast, faster than I ever imagined it could. But it has happened."

Lily didn't know what to say or do. She put her fork down unable to finish her breakfast, then rose to leave the table.

"Stop running from me, Lily. Stop running from yourself."

"I can't handle this. I'll meet you out front at 12:30."

Phillip watched her walk away, aching to go after her and sweep her up in his arms and take her to her room and make hot passionate love to her. He didn't understand his obsession with her. Then it dawned on him. He finally knew how Nicholas had felt when he was courting Camille and she'd repeatedly rejected him, denying her feelings and making them both miserable in the process.

Lily was doing the same thing to him.

He knew himself to be a disciplined, in control man. But around Lily he felt like a school boy with his first crush. He had to somehow exert more control over himself with her, and take it slow, giving her space and time to realize what they had was special and very precious. Not something to carelessly cast aside.

During the drive to the Quarter, Lily remained quiet. Phillip started up a conversation several times, but soon gave up when she continued to give him monosyllabic answers. He decided that if he were going to give her space, he should start now.

"The Puissant Contemporary Art Gallery is up ahead to the left."

Lily looked where he indicated. For the last few minutes her mind had been a million miles away. She now noticed that there were businesses of all kinds on the street. The colorful and diverse surroundings fascinated her.

Phillip pulled into the parking lot across from the gallery, got out and walked around to the passenger side to help Lily. He placed a protective hand at the small of her back as they crossed the street.

Lily took in at a glance the building's timeless multi- cultural ambiance. She could imagine the Spanish craftsmen at work creating the classic, lacy wrought-iron balconies. And she noted as well the strong French influence with its open air architecture, loggias and French doors made into the building itself.

The chime of the shop bell announcing their arrival and the delicate scent of jasmine greeted them.

"Phillip! It's so good to see you." A man of medium height with a diamond bright smile walked up to them. "Is this the lady I've been hearing so much about?"

"Lily, I'd like you to meet my friend, Henri Puissant. Henri, Lily Jordan."

To say Lily was shocked was an understatement. Henri Puissant's golden skin and grey eyes revealed his obvious mixed heritage. Those intelligent grey eyes had a perceptive almost clairvoyant look in them. It was as though he knew exactly how she felt about Phillip. And that was scary.

"You Cardoneaux brothers certainly know how to pick beautiful women."

"Considering how gorgeous your wife is, I'd say your taste in women equals ours. Where is the lady in question?

I called earlier to make sure she'd be home."

"Oh, Jolie is upstairs. Why don't you say hi to her and find out what she's cooking for dinner while I keep your beautiful water lily company."

"Don't complain when you come upstairs and find no dinner. I might just eat it all."

"If you do, let's just say that your pretty face may have to undergo unexpected plastic surgery when I'm done with it."

"Jolie's cooking makes the risk worth it."

Phillip sensed that Henri would help Lily over the awkwardness she was obviously feeling. She hadn't been able to hide her surprise at finding out he was not white. He smiled at Lily, then headed for the stairs leading to the Puissant's apartment.

"Did you know that Nicholas, Phillip's brother, has a few of his works on display at my gallery?" Henri asked.

"Yes. Phillip told me."

"Come, let me show them to you, Cherie."

Lily followed Henri into a room done in a light antique beige. There were blue and gold velvet drapes hanging at the windows and gold wall-to-wall carpet. She recognized a portrait of Magnolia Grove. She could feel the love the artist felt for the place in every brush stroke. Nicholas Cardoneaux was an extremely talented artist.

"Why were you so shocked to see me? Did you expect me to be white?"

This man was way too perceptive. "I just assumed–I'm sorry if I hurt your feelings."

"You didn't. My father was three quarters French and my mother is part black, Creole and Indian. What about you?"

"My father is white and my mother is black. Let me ask you something?"

"Go ahead."

"Do your parents get along? I mean do they love each other?"

"That's two questions. They did get along. My father died when I was fifteen. And yes they loved each other very much. I take it yours don't?"

Lily looked away and didn't answer."

Henri didn't pry, he showed her another of Nicholas's paintings.

"Jolie, whatever you're cooking smells wonderful," Phillip said as he walked into the Puissant kitchen.

"Phillip." She smiled. "I baked your favorite Peanut butter pecan pie."

"Pecan?"

"Oh, that's the new ingredient I've added to the recipe because I knew how much you like them. It was an experiment that worked and tastes delicious. Want to try it? I saved a little of the mixture just for you." She walked over to the refrigerator opened it and took out a container and carried it over to the kitchen table.

"I won't say no to that." He took the container and reached inside a drawer for a spoon.

"Something is bothering you, isn't it, Phillip?"

"You know me so well. I have a new lady in my life."

"And you've already fallen in love with her. Haven't you?"

"The problem is making her admit that she loves me too."

Phillip could feel Jolie's watchful gaze scrutinizing him. At that moment he believed that she had inherited her

Spanish Gypsy mother's fortune telling skills."

"I want to meet her. I have to see if she has good eyesight. Because you're wearing your heart on your sleeve. Surely she can see this."

"There's nothing wrong with her eyesight. She's attracted to me, more than attracted. The woman loves me. I know that. I feel it in my gut and most of all in my heart."

"There has to be a reason why she won't own up to it. And I think you know what it is."

"Lily has this thing about white men."

"Haven't you told her that you're not all white?"

"No."

"And why not?"

'It's complicated, Jolie."

"It's been a year since your mother dropped her bombshell on you and Nicholas. I know Nicholas has come to terms with the revelation and is on relatively good footing with your mother, but what about you, Phillip? How do you feel about it?"

He didn't answer.

"Are you happy, sad, angry, resentful? Proud, ashamed or what? You haven't really sorted out your feelings about that, have you?"

"No."

"I think you need to. Talk to Nicholas or if necessary get some counseling."

"I will–"

"But right now you want me to feel Lily out. Don't you?"

"Yes. I admit it. Since you come from a similar background and know what it's like to be a part of both worlds and I don't. I thought–you know."

"I understand. You've never had to personally deal with it until you met Lily. It's hard not knowing where you fit in, isn't it?"

"Yes, it is."

"You know, Lily may resent my intrusion into the situation. And you for inviting me to do so without discussing it with her first. Have you thought about that?"

"Yes."

"She may also resent you even more for keeping your heritage a secret whatever your reasons."

"I know I should tell her, but I want her to love me for myself. Can you understand that, Jolie?"

"You know I can and do, but you have to be prepared for the consequences of your actions. Or lack of them."

"You helped Nicholas with Camille."

"Yes. I did. And I'll help your Lily if she'll let me." Jolie took off her apron folded it and put it in a drawer, then smiled. "Let's go downstairs so I can meet your new lady friend."

Lily frowned upon meeting Jolie. She was still getting over the fact that the Puissants were a far cry from being what she had assumed they would be. By introducing her to them, was he in essence trying to show her that although he was white he had friends that were part black and she need not fear that he would take advantage of her.

Henri closed the gallery and they all went upstairs to have dinner. After dinner Phillip and Henri set up a table out on the balcony to play backgammon.

"Those two and Nicholas when they get together are really something else. They like doing what they call guy stuff." Jolie laughed.

"I understand. I have a friend, who also happens to be my photographer, and is the same way when he gets around his homeboys."

"You said he's your photographer. Are you a journalist?"

Lily laughed. "Oh, no. I'm a model."

Jolie looked her over. "I should have guessed. You're so tall and statuesque. Are you what they call a super model?"

"I'm afraid so. It doesn't bother you does it? I promise you I'm not a bad influence on children and old grandmothers."

"I like your sense of humor, Lily. Of course I'm not bothered. I figure that supermodels are people like everyone else. They may live a different lifestyle, but they are human too. How did you like the pie?"

"It was fabulous, Jolie. It makes me wish I could cook. Oh, I can do a few simple dishes, but not anything fancy. I mostly eat out or on the run from one photo shoot to another."

"It must get pretty hectic. How do you find time for yourself?"

"I haven't. That's the reason I'm staying at Magnolia Grove under Phillip's watchful eye. You see I collapsed on location in downtown New Orleans and was rushed to the city hospital."

"Since you're staying at Magnolia Grove you've met Phillip's mother."

"Oh, yes. I don't think she likes the idea of me staying there."

Jolie sighed and shook her head. "Around her son, you mean. Technically Magnolia Grove doesn't actually belong to her. Nicholas and Phillip share ownership. Their father left it to them in his will. Of course Suzette can live there for the rest of days or until she remarries. She's an expert at playing lady of the manor. That woman is a piece of work."

"Mrs. Cardoneaux and I have had a few touchy moments before she flew to Paris on her annual shopping trip."

Jolie laughed. "I bet you did. I've had quite a few touchy moments with her myself. It's probably been like a vacation for you with her gone?"

"I wouldn't say that exactly. Look, Jolie, I–"

"I understand. You don't want to say anything against her because she's Phillip's mother and you care for him. Believe me, I know of more pleasant topics of conversation than Suzette Cardoneaux. I'm only too glad to drop that subject."

Lily liked Jolie Puissant and her husband. They were good people. She remembered Phillip saying that he and his brother and Henri had been friends since they were little boys. Phillip was full of surprises evidently. What else would he reveal about himself? Things she would never have imagined probably.

"You and Jolie seemed to get along like a house on fire," Phillip said as they headed for Magnolia Grove.

"Yes. We hit it off. I like her. She's so down to earth."

"Like you. That pie was fantastic wasn't it."

She laughed. "You know it was. And that sautéed shrimp we had for dinner. You can't touch that. I can see why she's the head chef at Antoine's. I haven't eaten there yet, but I've heard of it."

"We can have dinner there anytime you want to go."

"I'd like that. You're not still upset with me, are you, Phillip?"

"I never was, just a little disappointed and a lot frustrated because you wouldn't make love with me. I want you so damned much I ache, Lily."

She knew what he was talking about because she wanted him just as much. But she would have to restrain herself. There could never be a future with him.

"Your brother is a talented painter. I loved the one he did of Magnolia Grove and the wharf."

"They are definitely works of art."

"You will be going back to work at the hospital tomorrow, won't you?"

"Yes. I wish I could spend more time with you. But duty calls. I'll try to get home early though. Anyway you can get more rest if I'm not around."

She started to say I'll miss you, but remained quiet.

CHAPTER ELEVEN

Phillip updated the information on his last patient's chart after finishing early morning rounds and handed it to Alice Clayborne.

"When did you go on the day shift, Alice?" he asked.

"Oh, it's only a temporary assignment, Dr. Phil. Betsy Metcalfe is off on disability and won't be back for at least a month. She sprained her back tangling with a new patient. I heard that it took two nurses and an orderly to subdue him after he'd suffered an adverse reaction to his medication. We asked him what medicines he was allergic to, but he hadn't known he was allergic to it because he'd never taken it before. Working around here is always educational even for me and I'm old as the—well we won't go into that," she quipped.

"Oh, you're not getting older, only better, Alice. I think you can handle anything that comes along," he said wryly.

"What about your other patient, Lily Jordan? Is she recovering all right?"

"She progressing nicely, Alice."

"I don't see why she wouldn't when she has you for her doctor."

"Thank you for the compliment."

"It's not a compliment, it's only the truth, Dr. Phil. This hospital is damned lucky to have you. Well, I'd better go and show the new student nurses the correct way to make a patient's bed."

"Carry on, Alice!" Phillip shook his head as he watched her march down the hall like a drill sergeant ready to give her regiment hell. Alice Clayborne would never change."

"Did the time off work for you, Phil?" Larry Mayfield asked walking up to the nurses' station.

"Oh, yes."

"I take it you got to at least square one with Ms. Jordan? That was the point of having her come live with you. Right?"

"She's not exactly living with me. At least not the way you're making it sound."

"Tell the truth. Am I exaggerating about your feelings for her?"

"I'm pleading the 5th on that one."

"Gaby was right. She said when you found the right woman she would knock you side ways. I think Ms. Lily Jordan has you down for the count."

"At least," Phillip answered. What he hadn't said was that he'd completely lost his heart to her and he didn't think he would survive if she didn't return his feelings.

"So when's the party?"

"Party? Oh, yes. I don't know, Larry. I'll have to get back to you about the date."

"Good enough. I'll pass the info on to my wife."

Lily sat lazing around the pool several afternoons later thinking about Phillip and their visit with Jolie and Henri. She was sure he had chosen Jolie in particular to talk to her because she and Lily came from a similar background. And hoped that she would convince her to change her mind about him. She did enjoy talking to the other woman. She sensed a fellow soulmate. She wanted to know more about Jolie's life. Maybe she would give her a call and they could have lunch or go shopping or something.

"That tan you have is the bomb, Lily pad."

"It's my natural color as you well know. I'm glad to see you, Carey. How did you know I'd be down here?"

"My man Edwards told me."

"Your man Edwards?" She laughed.

"Yeah. He didn't seem as freaked out by my appearance this time. You think he could be mellowing?"

"Maybe. I don't know. Hey, why don't you change into a pair of swimming trunks and we can take a soothing dip in the pool."

"I was afraid you'd never ask."

"Afraid? You? Carey Graham? I don't think so.

Listen, have you talked to Chris lately?"

"No. Why?"

"Nothing. I just asked."

"You don't ever just ask about anything, Lily pad. You had a reason. Spit it out."

"Don't you think she's cute?"

"I guess so." His eyes narrowed. "Wait a minute. Don't tell me you're going in for matchmaking?"

"Well, I think the two of you would look good together."

"You *are* matchmaking. I think charity should begin at home."

"What do you mean?"

"You know what! With Dr. Phil, as his patients so lovingly call him. Even that nurse from hell thinks he can walk on water. The point I'm trying to make is that the man is obviously besotted. But have you let him know that the feeling is mutual? I doubt it."

"Even if it was there can be nothing between us."

"Because he's white? That won't wash, Lily pad. He's nothing like that scumbag, Davies. And I think you know that. If you don't you should. You're falling for Dr. Phil. No, not just falling. You've already fallen."

"You don't know what you're talking about."

"I think I do. Now about Chris—I never considered her until now. Come to think of it every time I'm around she flashes me a pretty white smile."

"Don't play with her, Carey."

"I won't. You've got me interested so don't bail on me now. It's good to know that you and I are on the same page about something. Look, I'm going to the pool house and change. Be prepared to swim when I come out. I might even race you. And who do you think will win?"

Carey was as arrogant and macho as ever, she thought watching him swagger down the walk to the pool house.

Suzette Cardoneaux watched Lily and Carey from behind a hedge. The little tramp had the nerve to bring her trashy friends to Magnolia Grove. Well she wouldn't have it. She'd decided to come back early from her annual shopping trip. She hadn't really wanted to leave Phillip at the woman's mercy, but he had insisted.

She'd had Kyle Barnette do some checking on Lily's background. She was obviously part black. Suzette flinched. So was she, but that was different. Anyway it didn't matter what race the woman was from, she couldn't begin to be worthy of her son. He was much too good for someone like her. She was a model for goodness sake. Not just any model, but a supermodel.

Suzette was meeting Kyle tomorrow at Commanders for the results of his little investigation. She was sure he had found out something she could use to get her unwanted guest to leave Magnolia Grove. If Lily Jordan thought she was going to get her hooks into her son, she had better think again.

"We had a secret admirer, I see," Carey said as he trailed the lone figure's progress back to the house.

"Secret admirer?" Lily asked drying her hair.

"Going there." Carey pointed her out. "She's a jazzy looking woman. Is she Dr. Phil's mother by any chance?"

"That's her all right. She must have decided to cut her trip short. Can't leave her precious son in the clutches of a scandalous supermodel for too long. She was no doubt afraid I'd corrupt him."

"I see. You two get along like oil and water. I'd like to meet the Dragon Lady."

"Trust me, you don't want to do that, Carey."

"I like slaying dragons. Don't you know?"

"Not this one. You wouldn't stand a chance. She breathes fire and she'll fatally scorch you."

He grinned. "Not if I'm wearing fireproof armor."

Lily wondered why Suzette had been spying on them. The woman evidently had an agenda. And she was sure it wasn't a particularly nice one.

"Well, do I get an intro?" Carey asked.

"All right. Get dressed and meet me at the house. Your man Edwards will show you in. I'll alert him that you will be coming to the house after you've changed."

"Maybe once the old girl and I get acquainted, she'll give me permission to take some pictures of the estate. I know the perfect place to submit them."

"She's definitely not an old girl. I'm sure she wouldn't appreciate hearing you saying that. Oh, and about the pictures, Carey, don't count your chickens. Okay?"

"Gotcha, Lily pad. Just get me that intro, I'll take it from there."

"Remember, you asked for it."

Lily spotted Suzette sitting on a lounge chair on the terrace, thumbing through a society magazine.

"I'm curious, Mrs. Cardoneaux," Lily said as she stepped onto the terrace.

"Oh," she answered, looking up from the magazine, "about what?"

"I think you already know. Why were you spying on me and my friend a while ago?"

"I wasn't spying. Just curious. You are a guest at Magnolia Grove. And you should remember you are only here because my son took pity on you. That's the kind of man and dedicated doctor he is."

"You're right it is. The fact that he took me in as you put it isn't what's worrying you, though is it?" She longed to tell her what Jolie had revealed to her, that Suzette didn't really own Magnolia Grove and it was Phillip's hospitality she Lily was enjoying, but no matter how rude the woman could be, she would never say that to her.

Edwards showed Carey out onto the terrace, then left.

"Carey. I'd like you to met Mrs. Suzette Cardoneaux, Phillip's mother. Mrs. Cardoneaux, Carey Graham." Lily waited with baited breath for her reaction.

Suzette screwed up her lips in a derisive yet polite condescending smile as she took in Carey's appearance.

"Are you and Lily engaged?"

"No. I wish. Not for real. We're just friends. Tell me, Mrs. Cardoneaux, would you be willing to let me take a few pictures of Magnolia Grove. You see, I'm a professional photographer."

"Really. What magazine do you work for?"

"I free-lance when I'm not working for the Carlyle Modeling Agency."

"I see. Well, I don't think it's in the best interest of the Cardoneaux image to let you exploit it. You understand."

"Oh, yes. I understand all right. It's hard to believe Dr. Phil is your son." He smiled at Lily. "I'll get with you later, Lily pad." His eyes narrowed when he looked at Suzette. "I'll see myself out."

"Of all the—"

"You are unbelievable, Mrs. Cardoneaux."

"Coming from you I'm sure that's not meant to be taken as a compliment. My son wouldn't appreciate hearing you talk to his mother in that derogatory tone."

"Oh, I'm sure he knows first-hand how truly unbelievable you are."

"And what are you? A trashy little tramp that parades her body in front of the world pretending that it's a respectable profession. My son doesn't need your kind of woman except for physical gratification."

"How would you know what kind of woman I am? I'm not ashamed of what I do. Have you ever heard the saying that you shouldn't judge a book by the cover, Mrs. Cardoneaux?"

"I've heard of it. Your cover is as transparent as glass."

"And you think you know what lies between the covers. What exactly are you saying?"

"Yes. Mother, what exactly are you saying?" Phillip said striding toward them.

CHAPTER TWELVE

"Phillip! What are you doing home?"

"I do happen to live here, Mother. What were you and Lily talking about?"

"It wasn't important."

"Oh, I think it was."

"Phillip, your mother was—"

"Being her usual pleasant self? Is that what you're going to tell me, Lily? If you are, I'm not buying it." He glowered at his mother. "I warned you that if you upset or insulted Lily, you would answer to me. I meant what I said. If you say or do anything else to hurt her—"

"You'll what? Abandon me like your brother did?" She glared at Lily and stormed off the terrace into the house.

"Please, don't fight with your mother over me," Lily pleaded.

"What she said goes deeper than you know, Lily." He wondered if now was the time to reveal their heritage. No.

He'd wait until after he talked to Nicholas.

"Look, Phillip, I'll be gone in a few days."

"No. You won't, Lily."

"I will."

"You can't, I won't let you walk out of my life."

"You don't have a choice. I've decided to move to my hotel apartment. So don't fight with your mother on my account."

Phillip pulled Lily into his arms. "You're a part of my life now, Lily."

"A very small insignificant part in comparison to the rest of it according to your mother. It just wouldn't work between us. We're too different and I don't mean just the difference in our races. It's everything. You're a doctor and I'm a model. We're from opposite ends of the spectrum. Don't you see that?"

"Opposites do attract."

"Phillip, please don't."

"Don't what? You care for me, Lily. You more than care. Please, don't turn your back on what we could be to each other. You have hang-ups, I understand that. We all do, but I'll help you get over yours, sweetheart."

"Don't call me that, please."

Phillip kissed her gently, tenderly on the lips again and again.

"Oh, Phillip, when you do that I–I–"

"You what?" he said kissing her again.

Lily responded with sweet abandon when he caressed her breasts through the thin wrapper covering her bikini.

Suddenly his cell phone rang breaking the spell. He eased away from Lily and lifted the phone from his jacket pocket.

"Cardoneaux. What are his vital signs? And? All right. All right. Tell him I'll be there as soon as I can get there. Right."

"You have to go back to the hospital."

"I'm sorry. I'll try to get back as soon as I can. We have to talk."

"Phillip, I don't think–"

"Save it, Lily. We are going to talk."

She was trembling from that last kiss. Her body tingled with desire, refusing to calm down. It craved release from the tension and unsatisfied sexual frustration strumming through it. She hated to think what would have happened if he hadn't got that phone call. It was becoming increasingly difficult to resist Phillip, but she had to somehow find the strength to keep on doing it until she left Magnolia Grove. She had only a few days to go, but they would be the longest ones she would ever have to endure. God, help her she wanted to give in and let him make love to her. She knew it would go beyond physical satiation between them; even beyond rapture.

Phillip was exhausted by the time he returned to Magnolia Grove. All he wanted to do was shower and fall into bed. That wasn't exactly true. He wanted to go to Lily's room and make love to her until midnight met the dawn, but physically he just couldn't do it right now.

As he showered he remembered the feel of her soft luscious body pressed against his and he felt himself harden. He turned on the cold water in an attempt to tamp down the throbbing in his loins, his entire body. All he got was chilled. Lately he'd been walking around in a semi aroused state most of the time. Larry had kidded him saying it wouldn't be long before he was sending out wedding invitations.

He recalled the conversation he'd overheard between his mother and Lily and he got angry. His mother was interfering in his love life the way she had his brother's. Only this time it wasn't about the fact that she was black. She'd taken it into her head that Lily wasn't good enough for him and that made him even angrier. How dare she sit in judgment of Lily.

The next morning as Phillip waited for Lily to come to breakfast, his mother entered the room.

"Phillip, you must listen to me. That woman is not the right one for you."

"And you have Miss Right waiting in the wings?"

"Don't be disrespectful. Of course I don't, but I know that Lily Jordan is all wrong for you."

"How do you know that?"

"She's a model for God's sake."

"And that automatically makes her wrong for me?"

"You know what kind of life people like her lead. She's hardly suitable to be the wife of a brilliant young doctor."

"I'd say that was up to me to decide. I happen to think she is right for me. And if you interfere you won't like the consequences."

"Are you threatening me?"

"No. If you want to keep the peace between us, you'll rethink your attitude and try to get along with Lily." He looked up and smiled when he saw Lily. "I thought I would have to come get you."

Suzette glared at them both, but said. "If you'll excuse me.

"Remember what I said, Mother."

With her head held high, she left the room.

"Sit down, Lily."

"Do I need to ask what that was all about? I thought you'd already left for the hospital."

"I told you we needed to talk. I have time before I have to leave. What happened between you and my mother?"

"Oh, she was just being her usual sweet self."

"I gathered as much. Now tell me exactly what was said."

"Phillip, I don't see the point. You know that your mother hates me. It was just more of the same."

"There's more and I want you to tell me what it is."

"Why can't you just drop it?"

"I can't have my mother insulting you and not bring her to task about it. She'll begin to think she has a right to run my life. So far we've peacefully coexisted without any problems. I haven't had to insist that she stay out of my personal life before. But please don't misunderstand me. I'm my own man. And if she crosses the line I'll have to make sure she knows that I won't put up with it, mother or not. Are you listening to me, Lily?"

"But you and your mother are so close. I don't want to come between you."

Phillip took her hand. "Don't you think I know how manipulative my mother can be. I know she'll do most anything to get her way. I've ignored a lot of the things she has done in the past, but I won't where you're concerned."

At that moment Lily felt special. For this man to say what he had...

He's nothing like Kenton Davies or your father.

"I want you to meet my brother and his wife tomorrow evening."

"I don't know, Phillip."

"They'll love you, Lily. Then later we'll have a party and introduce you to more of my friends. We haven't had a party at Magnolia Grove in a long time."

"A party? But what about your mother? Surely she won't want to do that if it's for me."

"This is my home. If she won't cooperate, then I'll hire someone who will. Trust me, she'll agree."

Lily had her doubts about that. She was curious about his brother. And couldn't help wondering about the kind of person he was. He was obviously a very talented man. She wondered if it was a good idea to have a party. After all she'd be back in her apartment in a few days.

"So what do you say?"

"I—if you really want to do it."

"I do." Phillip glanced at his watch. "Look, I have to be going. We'll eat out this evening. At say seven? Remember if my mother says anything out of line. I want to know about it."

"I'll be ready."

Phillip kissed her gently on the lips. "Until this evening."

Lily hadn't seen Suzette at all that afternoon. She asked Edna where she was. She was told that Suzette had gone out. She was probably trying to avoid her. Talking to the older woman wasn't at the top of Lily's list either. But she'd decided to bury the hatchet for Phillip's sake. Now if Suzette would just meet her half way. Lily frowned. What were the odds of that ever happening?

Lily phoned Jolie and told her about Phillip's idea for the party.

"Now if we could just close his mother up in the basement..."

"Jolie."

"Just kidding."

"No, you weren't."

"I take it you and Suzette aren't exactly on good terms?"

"Huge understatement. She wants me gone."

"We can always hope she'll make herself scarce at the party. Or better still go back to Paris and finish her shopping."

"Not a chance. She'll come to the party if only to keep her eye on her son."

"You know I think she needs a man. No, seriously. I know how much she misses her husband. Phillip has told me this. If she had a man in her life she would stop interfering in her children's."

"It's been a while since he died, hasn't it?"

"Five years. The only man she sees socially is Kyle Barnette, the family attorney. Maybe I might just mention that to Phillip. I have to leave for the restaurant in half an hour. We'll talk again before the party. Henri and I are definitely not going to miss that great event."

"I'm glad. At least I'll have somebody there to lend me moral support."

"You'll have Phillip. And if I know Nicholas and Camille, they'll support you too."

"I hope you're right. I'm going to meet them tomorrow."

After hanging up with Jolie, Lily went to her guest suite to choose a dress for the evening. She felt relieved not to have to sit at the dinner table with Suzette

Cardoneaux. She was looking forward to spending time with Phillip.

CHAPTER THIRTEEN

"Commander's Palace is one of New Orleans's oldest restaurants according to what I've read," Lily said to Phillip as he drove through the Garden District.

"Read?"

"While I was still in the hospital, Carey brought me several magazines. One of them said that Commander's Palace made fine food an art. And that it began when they opened their doors in 1880. For a time that kind of dining had all but disappeared, but because of the Brennan family it has been restored."

"You have really taken an interest in our fair city."

"And a few of the people who live in it," she said flashing him a smoldering look, then changed the subject. "The homes we've passed are awesome. Is that Commander's Palace?"

Phillip gave her a smile that said he knew exactly why she had changed the subject.

"Yes. The architecture does remind you of a real palace, doesn't it?"

"Definitely. I feel like Cinderella must have when she entered the ballroom."

"What I have in store for you, my little Cindy, will make you feel like royalty."

"What do you have in store for little old me?"

"Come inside."

"Said the spider to the fly. Can't you give me a hint?"

"No," he answered when they drove up. A valet parking attendant approached and he handed him the keys and got out and walked around the car to open the door for Lily.

"Phillip."

"The palace awaits you, my princess."

Lily smiled. She loved seeing him like this. For this evening everything was right in her world. Could she conquer her fears and insecurities and let herself love this man?

You're already in love with him, girl.

A doorman splendidly dressed in a Victorian costume showed them inside the entrance hall. A maitre d' escorted them to the garden dining area.

"You have a thing for eating outdoors, don't you?"

"We can always go inside to one of the private rooms."

"No. I enjoy being in the garden."

He grinned. "You have to admit that it is beautiful out here."

"It certainly is. I'm afraid to ask what we're having for dinner."

"I've arranged for us to experience one of Commander's famous seven course meals."

"I can hardly wait."

She glowed with joy. God, her smile stole his breath.

Phillip was in a discussion with the wine steward about their choice when he saw his mother and Kyle Barnette being seated on the far side of the garden.

Lily followed Phillip's line of vision. "I talked with Jolie today and she said your mother and Kyle Barnette had been seeing a lot of each other. They've eaten dinner at Antoine's several time recently. You think there could be something going on between them?"

"It never occurred to me. She's been so miserable since my father died. Nicholas and I hoped that someday she would find someone." He was ready to believe it might be possible until he saw Kyle take a folder out of his briefcase and hand it to his mother. Knowing her it might be just business, but he had a feeling that it was about his business: namely Lily

Jordan. Surely after he'd warned her off she wouldn't have...

"Excuse me, Lily. I need to have a word with my mother." And with that he headed straight for her table.

"Mother, Kyle." Phillip observed the uneasy almost guilty look on the older man's face. "I didn't know you and my mother were seeing each other socially."

"Well, we—I mean."

"But this evening isn't really a social occasion, is it? What did she have you do, Kyle?"

Suzette cleared her throat. "Phillip, I—"

"I asked Kyle." Before the man could answer Phillip picked up the folder. It was labeled Lily Jordan in clear black letters. He scowled at his mother. "What is this?"

"You don't understand."

"Oh, I think I do. It's shades of Nicholas and Camille all over again, only worse; I'm your target this time. I told you not to interfere. I might as well have been talking to a brick wall. Will anything ever penetrate your defenses? I supported you when Nicholas refused to have anything to do with you after learning what you had done to us. Do you know how hard it was? Do you, Mother? I had compassion for what you'd obviously suffered all those years you kept your secret about being part black. I bent over backwards. I thought you had changed. I guess nothing will completely change what a person is inside."

"Phillip, my only motive is to make you see what kind of woman she is."

"Like you did with Nicholas about Camille. You're not God. What gives you the right? Because you're my mother? I'll see you in the morning. Tonight is for me and Lily. In the mean time you keep this, Kyle." He handed him the folder. "When I come to your office, don't tell me you can't discuss its contents with me."

"But, Phillip, I can't, not without your mother's authorization."

"Give it to him, mother."

"But—all right," she reluctantly agreed. "Go ahead, Kyle."

'I'm going back to my table now."

"Phillip, wait, I—"

Kyle put a hand on her arm. "Let him go, Suzette. He's angry right now. Tomorrow will probably be better. After he's had time to cool off."

"I only did it to save him from making another mistake."

"Be honest, Suzette. It wasn't your only reason.

You've got to curb your overprotective tendencies. He's a grown man. You nearly lost Nicholas. Do you want to risk losing Phillip?"

"No. Of course I don't. I just don't want to see him get hurt again. Gina Frazier almost destroyed him."

"I know, but you have to allow your children to make their own mistakes. No matter how painful that can be to watch. Anyway I didn't find out anything about Lily Jordan that would cause Phillip to lose interest in her."

"So I did it all for nothing. But then again maybe not. This is only the preliminary report. Right?"

"Yes. I don't like that look in your eye. Please, don't borrow trouble, Suzette."

Ignoring his plea she continued. "I want the final report sent to the house. There has to be something in it I can use."

Kyle shook his head.

Phillip returned to his table just as the dinner arrived.

Lily shot him a hopeful look. "Do you think it might be true?"

"What?" Phillip was so deep in thought it took a moment before what she said sank in.

Her expression altered. "Kyle Barnette is a lawyer. Is the reason they're together just about business?"

"You could say that. Let's enjoy this wonderful meal, then we can go listen to jazz at the Funky Butt."

"The what?"

"Don't be put off or scandalized by the name. It's a club that has one of the most soulful jazz atmospheres in New Orleans. You do like jazz, don't you?"

"Yes, I do."

"I'm in the mood for it tonight. Tonight is special."

"How so?"

"It's in appreciation of what you've done for me."

Lily tilted her head to one side. "What have I done?"

"You've made me realize that what I felt for Gina Frazier was superficial. What I feel for you is deep, Lily, and it grows deeper and stronger with each passing day."

"Phillip, you know that I–"

"Can't handle a committed relationship right now. I understand that, but, my darling tiger Lily, I'm willing to wait as long as it takes."

Lily picked up her fork and began to eat her shrimp cocktail. She wanted to say something to Phillip, but no ready answer came to mind. It was like he didn't expect one. She was getting in deeper and soon the situation would be way over her head. Like he said she wasn't ready and didn't know if she ever would be. Right now she was confused, her emotions were pulling her in two directions, and soon something would have to give.

As she watched him eat, she thought about his mother. She and Kyle Barnette had left almost immediately after their encounter with Phillip. Lily wondered if it had anything to do with her.

As for Phillip, he was trying to keep his face set in a relaxed neutral expression, but it was hard. He kept thinking about what his mother had done after he'd made it crystal clear that he wouldn't stand for her interference. He'd never really had reason to oppose her on anything–well that wasn't exactly true. He'd opposed her when he first started seeing Gina. Unfortunately she had been right about the woman. But she wasn't about Lily. She was nothing like Gina Frazier.

What was he going to say to his mother? Right now he was so angry, he knew if he spoke to her tonight he'd end up saying something that he might regret. He needed to talk about his feelings with someone who would understand and that person was his brother. It wasn't the only thing he needed to discuss with him. He'd call Nicholas–no he'd go to Cardoneaux Construction in the morning.

"Are you ready to go?" Phillip asked Lily when they'd finished their dinner.

"As soon as I've made a quick visit to the ladies' room."

Phillip watched her walk away. The sway of her hips was so seductive. And he noticed that heads turned when she passed by and jealousy slashed through him like a knife. He smiled to himself. He'd never known he could feel like this about any woman, especially after his last experience with one. He'd turned into a completely different kind of man since meeting Lily: an extremely jealous and possessive man.

At the club an hour later Phillip let the mellow jazz sounds enter his soul. As he danced with Lily, he was totally entranced by the wild gardenia scent she wore and her seductive womanly musk as they swayed in time to the beat.

Lily felt safe in Phillip's embrace. For the moment, those worries about him being white and her being black were held at bay. Their relationship wouldn't have to be like her parents'. There was hope that they–no she wasn't going to go there, not yet. She had time to sort it all out. Right now she would focus her attention on Phillip and just enjoy being with him.

CHAPTER FOURTEEN

"Phil!" Nicholas grinned as his secretary showed his brother into his office. He pushed away from his architect's easel. "To what do I owe this surprise visit? Not that any visit spur of the moment or any other kind isn't welcomed. You couldn't wait until this evening to see me. Huh?" When Phillip didn't smile, Nicholas told his secretary to bring in a pot of coffee and two cups.

"All right, as Hazel would say, spit it out."

"How is that great lady by the way?"

She's fine. I couldn't have a better mother-in-law. Now, let's get to the reason you came to see me."

"It's our mother."

"You don't have to say any more, I understand. What has she done this time?"

"She had Kyle investigate Lily's background after I expressly forbade it. Where does she get off playing chess with other people's lives?"

"I asked her the same thing once. The way she sees it it's a mother's duty to protect her children at all costs."

Phillip laughed. "It seems funny hearing you support her instead of me."

Nicholas added his own laughter to his brother's. "You're right it does. I understand her better now. I went to a couple of her support group sessions and gained insight into the root cause of her insecurities."

"If she'd only get a life."

"You been hanging around my brother-in-law?"

Phillip nodded. "Jamal has been doing some carpentry work on the new wing of the hospital for the last couple of months and we became friends. I guess he's kind of rubbed off on me."

"Getting back to our mother."

Phillip enlightened him about the confrontation between their mother and Lily and his conversation with Suzette and waited for a response.

"You're really serious about this woman, aren't you?"

"Yes, very serious. I'm in love with her, but there are problems."

"Maybe if you told her the truth about our family, our mother in particular."

"I know I should have, but–"

"But you haven't really come to grips with the reality yourself, have you? You should have gone to the support group counseling sessions with me and mother."

"I wonder how much they really helped her."

Nicholas took a sip of his coffee. "How exactly do you feel about being part black?"

"That's just it, I don't know."

"In theory we understand that we are, but we'll never really know what it's like to be black because we were raised as white. And the fact that we don't look black confuses the perception we have of ourselves."

"Lily has this deep-seated resentment toward white men, but even despite believing that I'm one of them, I think she's beginning to really care for me. If I told her the truth it might very well change her opinion, but damn it, Nick, I want her to love me Phillip Cardoneaux for the person I am. Finding out I'm part black has never really impacted me until I met Lily. It never occurred to me that the woman I care for would turn away from me because she believes I'm white. It's really kind of ironic, don't you think."

"Your situation is unique, little brother."

"Yes, it is. And I'll deal with the issue of how I fit into both worlds when I have to, but that's not the important thing right now. Mother's attitude toward Lily is. I don't know what else to do to impress on her that I mean what I say about her."

Nicholas studied his brother for a few moments before deciding to drop that subject.

"You said earlier you wished mother would get a life. Do you know something I don't?"

"I thought that she and Kyle–never mind it's obviously not true.

She's probably just using him."

Nicholas ran his fingers through his hair. "Maybe that's not all he is to her. She confided in Kyle during the first difficult weeks of her therapy when I couldn't bring myself to see her let alone forgive her. I know you were her rock, but Kyle is of her generation. And he's known her for quite a few years. I always secretly thought he was in love with her. When he first began representing Cardoneaux Construction, I sensed the attraction."

"You're right, Nick. Since Father's death he has been there for her. If she were to get involved with him, she wouldn't have time to meddle in my personal life."

"I wouldn't count on it. She's a woman who can do both, no problem."

"What is it about Lily that bothers her so much?"

"It's probably not about her personally, but what she represents. Mother sees Lily as a threat to you and she therefore needs to be eliminated. She feels guilty because she didn't do that with Gina Frazier."

"It doesn't excuse her treatment of Lily."

"No, but it explains her attitude. You're the last chick in the nest and she isn't ready to face the possibility of you leaving because she's terrified of being alone. She's hoping you'll find somebody and both of you will decide to live at Magnolia Grove."

"I'm a doctor, why haven't I seen that?"

Nicholas squeezed his shoulder. "You're too personally involved that's why. You know what's in your heart and mother doesn't. Don't let her bother you. Just keep on doing what you know is right for you. How does Lily feel about you?"

Phillip smiled. "I know she cares for me and I believe she may even be falling in love with me, but she has demons driving her and until she's faced them it's going to be rough going for a while."

"Are we Cardoneaux men fated to face challenges where our women are concerned?"

"Looks like it. I've always been the cool, calm and collected member of the family, but where Lily Jordan is concerned that doesn't apply."

"You're now officially a member of the club."

"I want you and Camille to come to the party. I'm shooting for next Saturday."

"That's only a few days away."

"The sooner the better. I'm hoping to convince Lily to stay a while longer. When mother realizes how perfect Lily is for me and how well she'll fit into my life, she'll back off."

Nicholas shot him a skeptical look. "That's hoping for a lot from her, don't you think? But don't give up hope. Mother and Camille seem to be getting along pretty well these days."

"Yes, they do. Then there may be hope for her and Lily?"

"Anything is possible. Without hope where would any of us be."

"I'm glad you're my brother, Nick." He gave Nicholas a bear hug. "I'll get back to you about the final details for the party. See you this evening."

When Phillip got home that evening his mother was in the living room waiting to talk to him.

"Well, aren't you going to say anything, Phillip?"

"We can talk later. Right now I have to shower and change. I'm taking Lily to meet Nicholas and Camille."

Phillip waited for her reaction. He could tell that she was itching to say something scathing about Lily, but thought better of it. He didn't know whether to feel relieved or suspicious.

Suzette cleared her throat. "Did you talk to Kyle?"

"Yes. Briefly."

"And?"

"I don't have time to discuss it right now. I told Nicholas that Lily and I would be there at seven. There will be plenty of time to discuss what Kyle and I talked about. Now, if you'll excuse me."

Lily had carefully selected just the right dress to wear to meet

Phillip's brother, Nicholas and his wife. It was one of her favorites—an ice blue, sleeveless evening dress with a matching butterfly embroidered tulle sleeved jacket. She chose blue strappy sandals to go with it. She'd modeled the outfit in Paris in the LaSalle spring collection for French Expressions.

She wanted to look her best for the coming meeting.

She'd decided to wear her hair in a slightly crimped hair style hanging down her back, and added sterling silver earrings and a chain around her neck to complement the outfit. As she sprayed perfume behind her ears, she couldn't help wondering what kind of person Nicholas Cardoneaux was. Surely he was like Phillip and nothing like their mother. A knock on the door scattered her reverie.

Phillip's breath caught in his throat, when Lily appeared. He hadn't thought she could look any better than she had in her black slip dress, but he'd been wrong. Talk about a vision of loveliness . . .

"What do you think?"

"Word's can't describe how fantastic you look, Lily."

She smiled. "Why thank you kindly, sir. Shall we go?"

Lily had read about the Lafayette district in the same magazine in which she had seen pictures of Magnolia Grove. It was considered an exclusive area. Cardoneaux Construction had built dozen's of homes there. Although the houses were elegant and cleverly designed, they didn't come close to Magnolia Grove's splendor. She wondered what made Phillip's brother move out of it. From all that Phillip had told her, Nicholas loved the magnificent mansion as much as he did. It must have been something pretty heavy. But then again most married men preferred not to live with their mothers.

Phillip stole quick glances at Lily as he drove, wondering what she was thinking. He smiled. It was something he found himself doing on a regular basis lately.

Lily gasped as they approached an elegant, aqua colored, two-story house. An alley of trees led up to the house. She had to admit that the grounds had been created by a landscape genius. Was it possible that Nicholas Cardoneaux had done it as well as designing this unique house? If he had to leave a place like Magnolia Grove, this house was definitely the one to soften the blow.

When they reached the house the driveway divided. To the left was a three-car garage and mini parking area. To the right a rose-trellised path trailed around the house through a magnificent garden. Although she hadn't even met Nicholas, she was already in awe of him.

As he watched Lily, Phillip sensed her appreciation of the sheer beauty of the place and wondered if knowing the whole truth about his family would alleviate her fears or make matters worse. Their relationship was still so new, he didn't want to risk jeopardizing it. In a way he was damned if he did or damned if he didn't tell her. One thing was sure. He would have to resolve the issue one way or another. And soon. There was no getting around it.

CHAPTER FIFTEEN

Lily didn't know what to expect when the door opened. She did a double take after it had. The resemblance between Phillip and Nicholas was striking. She had imagined they would look alike, but not this much.

"You must be Lily Jordan. I'm Nicholas," he said extending his hand.

Lily shook it and smiled. "I'm pleased to meet you."

"Where is the love of your life?" Phillip asked.

"Oh, she's putting the twins to bed. She'll be here in a few minutes."

Lily silently admired the house as they followed Nicholas into the living room. She'd never seen anything like it. The creative use of circular windows was fantastic. A welcoming feeling of warmth greeted her.

The portrait over the fireplace immediately caught her eye. It was of a pregnant black woman. Just as she was about to ask about it, the subject of the painting walked in.

Phillip smiled. "Lily, I'd like you to meet Camille, the best sister-in-law in the world. Camille, Lily Jordan."

"I've heard so much about you from Phillip. I feel as though I already know you. I'm sorry I'm late, but my children decided that tonight they wanted to extend their bath time."

"I wish I'd been there to watch," Phillip quipped.

"As you may have already guessed my brother-in-law adores his niece and nephew. I told him that he'd probably end up having a whole house full of children. Of course he has to find the right woman to make his dream come true."

Lily gave her a half smile. Could Camille possibly be hinting that she might be that woman.

Phillip observed Nicholas studying Lily all through dinner as if whatever he'd gleaned had confused him. And Lily was quiet and reserved after looking at the pictures of Xavier and Solange. He wondered if she liked children. He hoped she did because like Camille had said he wanted a whole house full. He was getting ahead of himself. He'd only recently advanced to square three with Lily. There was still the matter of telling Lily about his heritage.

As they relaxed in the living room after dinner, the subject of Camille's portrait came up.

"Nicholas painted it just before our wedding," Camille explained. "As you might have guessed I was less than elated to be painted in my advanced stage of pregnancy."

"You said before the wedding? I don't understand?"

"Our situation was unique," Nicholas related. "You see Camille and I met at the Hadley Fertility Clinic. Because of a mistake we discovered that instead of being inseminated with her late husband's sperm, Camille had been inseminated with mine. My former wife Lauren had conceived and then miscarried Camille's husband's child. Needless to say all manner of complications arose from the clinic's mistake."

"The babies brought us together, but love keeps us that way." Camille smiled at Nicholas.

Lily shot them both a skeptical look. They made their relationship sound so perfect. She knew better. Of course they wouldn't reveal any problems they may have. Her parents had been experts at hiding theirs from the world. Only she knew the truth because she had lived under the same roof. Lily glanced at Phillip. He evidently thought that by meeting his brother and sister-in-law she would be convinced that they could work things out. That all interracial marriages didn't all turn out the way her parents' had. What about the children? They were only babies now. But what would happen once they were older and more aware of things. Would being of mixed racial heritage eventually cause them serious problems?

Phillip sensed the tension in Lily. He hoped she wasn't angry with him for his two-fold purpose in bringing her here.

"I'm looking forward to the party," Camille commented.

"So am I," Nicholas added. "It should be interesting."

Phillip smiled and said to Lily. "You've already met Jolie and Henri. At the party you'll get to meet some more of my friends. They're going to love you as much as I—"

Xavier and Solange chose that moment to run into the room.

"Unca Pip!" Solange exclaimed launching herself into her uncle's lap. He wrapped his arms around the little girl and then kissed her fat cheeks.

Xavier toddled over to Lily and gazed curiously at her.

Lily looked from one twin to the other and then rose abruptly to her feet. "I think we had better go and let Nicholas and Camille put their children to bed."

Nicholas and Camille locked gazes with Phillip.

As Phillip drove back to Magnolia Grove taking the river route, Lily focused her attention on the river.

"What's wrong, Lily?"

"Nothing is wrong. Why do you ask?"

"After the twins entered the room you turned cold and distant all of a sudden."

"I don't like being manipulated, Phillip. I told you that there can never be anything permanent between us."

"Lily, I know you're disillusioned by the relationship between you and your parents. And I thought that if you met Nicholas and Camille you would see that it could be different for us."

"You took me to met Jolie and Henri for the same reason."

"I was sure that Jolie could help you put things in the proper perspective. Is that so terrible, Lily?"

"I really don't feel like discussing this right now. Maybe having a party in my honor is a bad idea."

"I don't agree. I want my friends to meet and get to know you."

"You haven't been listening to me, Phillip."

"When you say something I want to hear then maybe I will."

Lily glared at him. Penetrating his stubbornness was like trying to drill a hole into a slab of granite with a Q-tip. The man was impossible.

Phillip smiled at Lily's frustrated expression. He intended to marry this obstinate woman and have a house full of children with her. He would settle for nothing short of his dream of love and happiness.

When Phillip came home from the hospital the next day, he found his mother alone in the living room. He knew he couldn't put off their inevitable confrontation about Lily any longer.

Judging from the expression on her son's face, Suzette knew what was coming.

"We may as well get on with it, Phillip."

"Where is Lily?"

"According to Edna, she went out earlier to meet one of her friends and hasn't returned."

Phillip let out a tired sigh. "All right, Mother, I want to know why after emphatically suggesting it, you went against my wishes and had Kyle investigate Lily?"

"I did it for your own good. The woman is not good enough for you."

"You didn't think Camille was good enough for Nicholas either. But you were proven wrong just as you will be about Lily."

"She has completely blinded you to her real character."

"And you think you know her real character?"

"There's no reasoning with you."

"Not where Lily is concerned. I want to throw a party to introduce her to my friends. And I want you to organize it."

"You what? Knowing how I feel about her? You expect too much, Phillip."

"I don't believe I do. And if you refuse to do this, I'll—"

"You'll what?"

"I'll hire a catering service."

"No, don't. I'll arrange it. Just tell me what kind of theme you want."

"Why are you suddenly being so cooperative?"

"If I oppose you on this, you'll only dig your heels in deeper. I see that you're going to have to find out for yourself what that woman—"

"Her name is Lily, Mother. I hope you change your attitude about her because if you don't, it won't be very pleasant around here."

"What do you mean?"

"I'm going up to shower before dinner. When Lily gets back be civil to her. Please?"

"Lily, I'm glad you called. Do you need me to do anything for you?" Chris asked as she and Lily had coffee and beignets at Café du Monde.

"No. Phillip is determined to give a party to introduce me to his friends. I met his brother and sister-in-law last evening."

"You didn't like them, did you?"

"It's not a matter of liking or disliking them. They were just a complete surprise."

"In what way?"

"They're an interracial couple."

"I see." Chris hesitated. "Look, I know since your experience with Kenton Davies you've avoided interracial relationships like the plague. Is there something more about this couple that bothers you? Do they in some way remind you of your parents?"

"Not exactly. I don't know them well enough to form an opinion."

"They wouldn't happen to have children, would they?"

"Yes. They have twins, a girl and a boy."

"You see yourself in them, don't you? You never said, anything, but I take it that your childhood wasn't a particularly happy one."

"No, it wasn't."

"But this couple is a part of Phillip's family. If you're interested in him, you'll have to—"

"I know that, Chris. I didn't intend for my relationship with Phillip to go beyond—"

"Beyond what? Friendship? Lily, Lily. Don't you know that you have no control over who you fall in love with. Or any guarantees that it'll work out. Haven't you told me that often enough?"

"Yes, I have. I may not have control over love, but it's my decision as to whether or not I'll do something about it. Let's change the subject. This isn't why I asked you to meet me. The last time I spoke to Carey you were all he could talk about. I believe you've made quite an impression on him, girl."

"I never thought you'd actually talk to him about me."

"I didn't have to say that much. He said you have a pretty smile and that he's definitely interested. I want you and Carey to come to the party. It's the perfect vehicle to get things moving. So will you come?"

"Of course. I can't pass up a chance to wow a certain male. You've got to go shopping with me. I've found this wonderful boutique called Deja's."

"All right, I'd love to. I'll be needing a special outfit for the party."

Lily had purposely lingered in New Orleans hoping to avoid having to talk to Suzette Cardoneaux any more than was necessary. She also hoped that Phillip wouldn't be home in time for dinner and she could have it in her room.

The last thing she wanted to do was rehash their discussion about his manipulation and expectations about her meeting with his brother and sister-in-law. Meeting them hadn't changed her opinion one bit. She still wasn't going to get involved with him.

Lily knew she had hoped in vain when she entered the living room at Magnolia Grove. Phillip and his mother had evidently waited dinner for her. She couldn't help feeling uncomfortable when Suzette smiled at her. The woman was obviously relishing her discomfort.

During dinner Phillip watched the silent exchange between Lily and his mother. He didn't like it and he planned to put a stop to it.

"Mother, Lily, I was thinking that we should have a jazz theme for the party."

"I like the idea. I really enjoyed myself the other night at the jazz club."

Phillip smiled. "You have your theme, Mother. This coming Saturday is the best day to have the party."

"But it's such short notice."

"Lily and I will give you our guest lists in the morning. I've already mentioned to just about everybody I plan to invite that it would be soon. All you need to do is call them to confirm the exact date and time. You can always hire additional help."

Phillip said to Lily. "I know you'll want to invite Carey Graham and your friend Chris?"

Suzette gasped. "Have you seen that man? Surely you're not going to invite him!"

"Don't be such a snob, Mother. Of course we're going to invite him. He's a friend of Lily's and is always welcome here."

"But, Phillip—"

"Mother."

"Very well." Suzette rose from her chair. "If you'll excuse me. I'll say good night."

"I can tell she's not eager to see Carey again. I don't blame her after the things she said to him. And what he said back to her." Lily reflected on the encounter.

"It should prove to be an interesting party. I have early morning rounds so I'll walk you to your room."

The next morning Lily hurried to the terrace to have breakfast with Phillip before he went to the hospital. Instead she found his mother eating alone and started to go back to her room, but she stopped. She'd make an effort to be nice to the woman for Phillip's sake.

"Phillip left for the hospital a few minutes ago," Suzette volunteered.

"Do you mind if I join you?"

"Since Phillip is not here, I have to wonder why you would want to."

"Mrs. Cardoneaux, please. I don't want to fight with you," she said easing into a chair across from Suzette.

"What you want is my son. Why don't you leave and go to your own apartment."

"I'm not looking to get involved with Phillip. He's my doctor and I like him."

"And there is nothing going on between you? Ms. Jordan, I'm not a fool. By playing hard to get you insure his continued interest in you. An experienced woman like you knows how to use that to her advantage."

"Look, I've tried to get along with you for Phillip's sake. I've evidently been wasting my time." She stood up. "You don't have to worry anymore, I'm leaving, Mrs. Cardoneaux."

Tears stung Lily's eyes as she headed for the guest suite. She couldn't understand how anyone could be so hateful. Once she reached the guest suite, she started taking her clothes and shoes out of the closet. She pulled her suitcase down from a shelf in the closet and began packing. After a few minutes she stopped to catch her breath. And suddenly feeling dizzy, she sank down on the lounge by the French doors. She would rest for a few minutes then she could finish packing.

Phillip came home early so he could spend some time with Lily. Eager to see her, he went straight to her room, taking the garden path. The French doors were open and Lily lay asleep on the bed. His smile faded when noticed her clothes draped across the back of the lounge and her half-filled suitcase on the seat. She'd obviously been packing and the exertion had tired her out.

Why was she leaving without telling him? She still wasn't completely recovered. His mother was no doubt responsible. He walked over to Lily and sat on the bed and gently shook her awake.

"Phillip!"

"How do you feel?"

"I'm fine."

He waved his hand. "What is all this?"

"I was packing. It's been almost two weeks since I came here. I think I'm recovered enough to move back to my hotel apartment."

"I don't happen to agree with your diagnosis, Dr. Jordan."

"Phillip—"

"Packing tired you to the point where you had to lie down. Doesn't that tell you something? Does my mother have anything to do with your decision to leave?"

She didn't answer.

"I thought so. Look, Lily, I offered you a place where you could regain your health. This house is mine and I can invite whomever I please to stay as long as I wish them to. I don't want you to go, tiger lily."

"But your mother—"

"I'll have a talk with her later. Right now all I'm interested in is convincing you stay." He bend and kissed her lips. When he heard her moan, he kissed her throat and caressed her breasts.

"Oh, doctor, you're taking unfair advantage."

"All's fair in love and war."

"Phillip, you have to stop."

"Why?" He kissed her again and again."

"All right, I'll stay for a few more days, at least until after the party."

"Nothing like friendly persuasion."

"I'd say your brand of persuasion is a little more than friendly, doctor."

"Oh, so you like my bedside manner?"

"It has a lot to recommend it."

Phillip stroked her cheek and kissed her again, then eased off the bed. "Now I want you to rest. That's doctor's orders."

Lily yawned. "Yes, sir, I hear and obey."

"I'll have Edna come in later and hang your clothes back up. We'll dine together on your terrace at seven," he said heading for the door.

Phillip went in search of his mother and found her in her sitting room.

Suzette looked up from the book she'd been reading. "I don't have to guess why you're here."

"Mother, Lily is a guest in this house, my guest. She's here to recuperate at my behest. She's not as strong as she likes to think. Packing to leave nearly wiped her out."

"I suppose you convinced her to stay."

"I'm very angry with you right now. Please understand this. Lily is staying until I deem she's well enough to go. Do I make myself clear?"

"Phillip, I—"

"Not another word. I'll expect you to at least be civil to my houseguest. To expect you to be friendly would be asking too much." With that he strode from the room.

CHAPTER SIXTEEN

"I saw the decorations. Your mother certainly knows how to organize a party on short notice," Lily commented to Phillip as they admired the ballroom the afternoon of the party.

Phillip was thoughtful as he looked around. When his father was alive they'd given parties all the time. Since his death they had been rare and rarer still after his brother moved out.

"Phillip."

"Yes. I'm sorry, I was thinking about my father just now. God, I miss him."

Lily remained silent. A frisson of guilt slid down her spine. Her father was alive, but she rarely saw him and only when pushed to do so. She reached for a change of subject.

"I'm glad your sister-in-law agreed to play the piano this evening. Jolie told me that she used to perform concerts and even went on tours."

Phillip wondered if Lily was sincere about Camille or was just being polite for his benefit. He got the feeling that she didn't exactly approve of his sister-in-law. He should have told Lily the truth so she wouldn't have been shocked when she met Camille. When she finally found out he wasn't what she thought he was, he knew he would be in trouble. She would be angry and feel that he'd lied to her even if it was only by omission.

"I think you should take a nap so you'll be fresh for the party," Phillip suggested.

"Yes, sir." She saluted him.

"Did that sound like an order?"

"Around the edges, but it's all right. You were just being you. You can't help it."

"I'm glad you understand me so well."

"You're right as usual. I am a little tired. The excitement and the last minute shopping has sapped my energy."

"I am looking forward to showing you off, lady. Can't have you sporting bags under those beautiful eyes now can I?" He teased.

"That definitely won't do. I want to be the bell of the ball so to speak."

"Oh, you will be."

"I'm glad that Carey and Christine will be there. I won't feel like a stranger."

"You know Jolie and Henri. And you met Nicholas and Camille." Phillip frowned. He noticed the slight alteration in Lily's expression when he mentioned his sister-in-law.

"Don't worry. I'll be there by your side just call on me."

"That sounds vaguely familiar. Like a love song from the 70s. I even remember who sang it. It was Marvin Gaye and Tammy Terrell."

"Lily."

"I know, nap time. Nag, nag, nag."

"Only because I care, tiger Lily."

"All right, I'm going."

Phillip smiled as she left the room.

Lily held the dress she'd bought at Deja's against her body as she stood in front of the mirror in the guest suite sitting room. The poppy red color complimented her golden brown skin and dark honey blonde hair. She remembered when she was eight how she hated the color of hair and wished it were black like her mother's.

She recalled the time she and her mother and father went to visit his relatives in the small Georgia town of Caprice. She was made to feel uncomfortable as well as unwanted by her Aunt Holly who purposely ignored her and lavished attention on her all white nieces and nephews. She'd angered Lily's father with her attitude towards his wife and daughter and they'd never gone there again. She hadn't had any trouble in New Jersey because there people were too busy with their own lives and taking care of their own business to meddle in other people's. Nobody cared whether you were mixed or not. Her parents were too engrossed in their day to day battles with each other to notice how unhappy their daughter was.

That was a long time ago. She had survived and gone out on her own as soon as she could. Until she met Phillip she hadn't believed she could find a white man who would love her for herself. Her ex-boyfriend had enjoyed making love to her and being seen with a supermodel, but as far as marriage or a long term relationship was concerned he hadn't wanted that with her. He had told her that every white man was entitled to a taste of brown sugar. She believed that type of attitude had died, but Kenton showed her it hadn't completely.

Phillip was special. Although he desired her body, he cared for her, respected her and wanted a relationship with her because he genuinely liked her, hang-ups and all.

He more than likes you, girl and you know it.

She glanced at her watch, it was time to get dressed for the party.

"Your mother has gone all out for this party," Jolie commented to Phillip as she looked around the ballroom at the posters of Sarah Vaughan, Louis Armstrong, Ellis Marsalis and other jazz greats.

"Considering how she felt about and treated Lily, no one was more surprised than I when she told me she'd gotten the Elkins Jazz Quartet to perform tonight. I had let her know that her attitude was not acceptable and believe it or not she's been on her best behavior for the last few days."

"That's good. I know how much you care about Lily. When are you going to do something about it?"

"I plan to make her my wife in the very near future."

"What about your mother?"

"I hope she'll accept it."

"And if she doesn't?"

"Although I own this house, I would do what my brother did and move out. There's no way I'd sentence Lily to a lifetime of unpleasantness with my mother."

"And you told her this?"

"Not specifically."

"You can't be subtle with her. You know from past experience, excuse my French, that she can be a real bitch."

"You never pull any punches, do you, Jolie? That's what I've always liked about you."

"I'm glad it's only like and not anything else because if it was, in the old days, I'd have had to call you out, Cardoneaux."

"Henri, I was wondering where you were."

"I was talking to that very interesting man over there. The one sporting the platinum hair and wearing the distinctly, funky designer clothes. Where do you know him from?"

"That's Lily's photographer and friend."

Jolie laughed. "I bet his appearance here didn't win Lily any brownie points with your mother. I think he's cute."

"Jolie!"

"Not to worry, Henri. He's not as cute as you, sweetheart."

"Thanks, I think."

"You too are really something. It's time I went to see if our guest of honor is ready to make her grand entrance."

"Chris, how do I look?" Lily asked her friend as she turned this way and that in front of the mirror.

"I don't know why you're tripping. You know you look good in anything. That dress is the bomb. Deja Parker certainly knows her stuff. I love this dress she made for me. Carey was speechless when he came to pick me up."

"I told you once he realized how pretty you were, you wouldn't be able to get rid of him. According to what he told me yesterday, you two are a couple."

"We are. Thanks to you."

"I can't take all the credit, you did it yourself; I just helped a little."
They heard a knock at the door.

"Lily, are you ready?" Phillip called to her.

"Yes, come on in."

When he opened the door and saw her, he was momentarily over-come. "You take my breath away, Lily Jordan. How are you, Chris?"

"I'm good. Look, I'll leave you two alone and go find Carey. See you in a few."

"Just when I think you can't get any more ravishing you surprise me, tiger Lily."

"Flattery, doctor?"

"I'm just an ordinary man tonight."

"You'll never be just an ordinary man, Phillip."

"The thing is, will you let me be your special man."

"Phillip."

"I know, you're not ready." He held out his arm. "May I escort you into the ball, Cinderella?"

"Yes, my prince. All I need is a tiara."

CHAPTER SEVENTEEN

When Phillip and Lily entered the ballroom, they were greeted by a succession of flashing camera lights as Carey took pictures.

"May I present Lily Jordan our guest of honor," Phillip said proudly as he introduced Lily, a smile lighting up his face.

The Elkins Quartet played *You've Got Me under Your Spell* and Phillip and Lily were immediately surrounded.

Suzette Cardoneaux watched from her place by the French doors. Kyle Barnette sat next to her.

"She's even more attractive up close. The picture in her file doesn't do her justice," Kyle commented.

"All men ever see is the outside cover."

"Phillip evidently sees more than that in Ms. Jordan. That final report doesn't condemn the young woman. Only you are doing that, Suzette."

"Don't start preaching to me, Kyle. I don't want my son involved with that woman."

"I know you don't think she's good enough, but that's up to Phillip to decide."

"I don't want to talk about this anymore. All right? I have to get through the rest of the evening on my best behavior around that little——around that woman. I wanted you here for moral support which, judging from what you just said, you're not going to provide."

Hazel Parker walked over to them. "You did a wonderful job with the decorating, Suzette. Camille was touched when you asked her to play tonight."

"She's extraordinarily talented."

Hazel smiled. "How are you, Mr. Barnette?"

"I'm fine, Mrs. Parker. May I call you Hazel? And please call me, Kyle."

"Yes by all means, *Kyle*."

"Where are Nicholas and Camille?" Suzette asked.

"They were putting the twins to bed and said they'd be a little late."

Phillip saw Larry and Gaby Mayfield and guided Lily to where they stood talking as they looked up at a picture of Ella Fitzgerald.

"Lily, I'd like you to meet my friend and colleague, Larry Mayfield and his lovely wife, Gabrielle."

"Please, call me Gaby. Everyone else does."

"Pleased to meet you, Gaby. And you too Larry."

"I was told you were a model, but no one prepared me for such exceptional beauty," Larry replied, fixing his eyes on Lily.

"Thank you for saying that."

"It's only the truth, Ms. Jordan."

"Call me Lily."

Carey and Christine walked over to them. "This is one jammin' party, folks."

"I'm glad it pleases you," Phillip said. "I don't have to ask how you and Chris are doing."

"No, you don't. This is one together lady on top of being beautiful."

Phillip smiled. "We seem to be surrounded by beautiful women tonight."

The quartet began to play a smooth jazz number.

"Care to dance, Chris," Phillip asked.

"I'd love to."

Larry and Gaby followed them out onto the dance floor.

"Care to dance, Lily Pad?"

"Not right now, Carey."

"You're feeling okay, though?"

"Oh, yes. Let's go out on the terrace for some fresh air."

Once outside, Lily asked. "I hope you didn't have a confrontation with Suzette Cardoneaux when you arrived."

"No. The Dragon Lady didn't send any searing flames my way. I was surprised actually, considering our last meeting."

"Phillip is responsible for her changed attitude. She hasn't been openly hostile toward me, but I sense her dislike simmering beneath the surface. I'm so glad to have you and Chris here tonight."

"Have any of the other guests been—"

"Rude? Oh, no. Everyone has been nice. Henri said he'd talked to you."

"He's cool. I told him I'd like to display some of my work at his gallery."

"That would give your career a real boost. What you do with a camera is sheer artistry, Carey."

"You're my one woman cheerleading team, Lily Pad."

"Friends for life, remember? Phillips's brother, Nicholas, and his wife are late. I hope nothing is wrong."

"I'm sure they'll be here. If his brother is anything like Doc Phil, he's a cool dude. But then on the other hand if he's like that mother of theirs..."

"Yeah. I think we'd better go back inside. The song is about to end."

As Lily and Carey went back inside, several couples entered the ballroom. Phillip escorted Chris to Carey's side and seeing the couples, he smiled and guided Lily across the floor.

"My brother and Camille have finally arrived. I'm glad that Jamal and Deja decided to come tonight."

Phillip studied Lily's face and saw how her eyes narrowed when they settled on Camille, then went blank.

When they made their way to Nicholas and Camille's side, he felt Lily stiffen. What was going on?

"I was wondering whether you guys were going to make it."

Lily recognized Deja Parker. She'd bought the dress she had on at her boutique.

"It's nice seeing you again, Lily," Deja said with a smile. "This is my husband, Jamal."

He extended his hand. "Pleased to meet you, Ms. Jordan."

"Call me Lily."

"When you tried that dress on, I said to myself that dress was really you," Deja commented.

Lily smiled. "You do fantastic work, Deja. You're as good as, if not better than, many of the designer's clothes I've modeled."

"You're so nice to say that."

"It's true."

"I didn't know the two of you knew each other," Camille interjected.

"Oh, yes, Lily and her friend came to my shop the other day looking for something to wear for tonight. Not to worry,
I fixed them up right and tight."

Lily felt Nicholas's intense appraisal and wondered what he thought about her.

"Are the twins all right?" Phillip asked.

"They're fine. The reason we were late is that they just don't like going to bed."

"I remember when Nick and I were little we didn't either."

Camille's eyes widened. "Are you telling me it's hereditary?"

"We outgrew it, and look how great we turned out." Nicholas laughed.

Camille whispered in an aside loud enough for the brothers to hear. "You can tell these two are extremely modest."

"My dearest sister-in-law you wound me to the quick," Phillip said frowning in mock hurt.

Lily could feel the camaraderie between the brothers and with Camille. Nicholas and Camille seemed to have a special rapport that she found refreshing after witnessing the way her parents were with each other. She had a feeling that Phillip had purposely given this party not just to introduce her to his family and friends, but to show her that mixed couples don't necessarily get along like her parents had. She realized that he cared deeply for her, and his compassionate nature had moved him to try and help her overcome her hostility toward her parents.

Phillip took his sister-in-law's hand. "It's time for you dearest, Camille, to perform your pied piper thing."

"Pied piper thing?" Lily gazed questioningly at him.

"When this beautiful lady plays the piano she draws people to her like a magnet. Come and prove yourself," he said urging Camille toward the piano.

"You can tell my brother is a true fan," Nicholas said.

"Let's find a seat near the bandstand."

Minutes later Phillip joined them.

As they all listened to Camille play, Lily realized that she'd heard her style of playing before.

Guessing at her thoughts, Jamal said. "My sister used to tour the U.S., Europe and South America a few years ago. She recorded under Camille King," he said proudly.

To Phillip, Lily said. "You have a talented family."

"Want to become a member?"

Lily smiled and focused her attention on Camille. The questions she wanted to ask would have to wait.

Just as Camille finished, a pair of late guests arrived. The room turned deathly quiet for a few minutes before the Elkins Quartet started to play *I've Got You under Your Skin*.

Lily noticed the strained look on Suzette Cardoneaux's face and the cold look in Phillip's eyes. She frowned, wondering who the couple was standing in the archway.

"What's wrong?" she asked.

"She has a nerve coming here after what she did," Deja hissed.

"Who is she?"

"Gina Frazier," Nicholas answered. "I agree Deja. She does have a nerve showing her face here."

Camille joined them. "How did she find out about the party?"

"She happened to be in the Puissant Gallery when Larry and I were there talking to Henri," Gaby Mayfield answered. "It never occurred to me that she would crash the party."

Nicholas rose from his seat. "Maybe someone should–"

"No, big brother. If we all ignore her she'll get bored and leave."

Lily observed the woman scan the room as though looking for someone. She had auburn hair and distinctly Celtic features with leaf-green eyes. She had full lips that hinted of a sensual nature and a voluptuous body to tempt most men. She'd obviously attracted Phillip at one time. Instant jealousy streaked through Lily at the thought of him being in that woman's arms, making love to her.

A smile spread across Gina Frazier's face as she found the person she sought. She urged her companion forward. He had an uncomfortable look on his face but didn't resist.

"Phillip, it's been a long time, hasn't it, darling?"

"What are you doing here, Gina?"

"I heard you were throwing a party. Did you know that Gerald and I are divorced."

"Is that supposed to mean something to me?"

"Don't be rude, darling. I know I hurt you, but I want to make it up to you."

"You never could. I'd suggest that you leave."

"But Jack and I just got here. May I introduce Jack Olsen. He's an old school friend of mine."

Jack cleared his throat. "Gina maybe we should–"

"Don't be ridiculous, Jack."

Phillip could strangle Gina for coming here. This was supposed to be a party to introduce Lily to his friends and family not for her to be embarrassed or humiliated by his ex-fiancée.

Phillip grabbed Gina's arm and ushered her out onto the terrace.

"Why in the hell did you really come here, Gina? To see if I'm still pining for you? The answer is no. I've found that special someone. I used to believe it was you, but I was wrong."

"You mean that skinny half-black woman you were sitting next to? You must be desperate, Phillip."

"No. When I was with you I was desperate. I couldn't see the forest for the trees. And if you really want to know, I'm part black too. Does that turn you off, Gina?"

"Actually, it makes you more interesting. You know what they say about a man having a strain of black in his genes."

"You're really disgusting, Gina."

She slipped her arms around his neck. "You didn't think so when you were making love to me. I know you miss what we had."

"It's in the past. I've forgotten all about it."

Gina splayed her hands across the front of his pants and caressed him.

Phillip stepped back, appalled.

Gina laughed. "You're already becoming aroused, aren't you?"

"If I am it's not because of you."

"I don't believe you."

"Doesn't matter whether you do or not."

Lily joined them. "You owe me a dance, doctor," she said her voice husky. "And a whole lot more." She shot Gina a challenging look, daring her to say anything.

Evidently, for Gina retreat was the better part of valor.

She smiled. "I'll collect my dance later, my darling Phillip. Jack is waiting for me inside." With that she swept past them into the house.

"So that's the infamous Gina Frazier."

"I didn't invite her here, Lily."

"I know you didn't. The Gina Fraziers of this world don't wait for an invitation when they've decided they want to do something or go somewhere they're not wanted."

"Let's go back inside."

Smiling up at Phillip, Lily wrapped her arm around his. She'd overheard most of the conversation between him and Gina. It warmed her heart to hear him say she was special. He'd told Lily that, but to know he had said that to his ex...

She was beginning to believe that a relationship between them could actually work. Phillip would never use her the way Kenton Davies had. Still she thought about how her parents had gotten along. They probably had stars in their eyes when they met and thought once they got married love would perform miracles. That their different cultures would blend. But evidently they'd been wrong. Why else would they argue and bicker about everything? She just didn't understand why that was so. Maybe she never would, but her relationship with Phillip was different.

CHAPTER EIGHTEEN

Obviously realizing she wasn't making any progress, Gina and her friend left the party early. Lily smiled. The other woman wanted Phillip, but he'd made it crystal clear that he wasn't interested. Not that that would stop or slow the voluptuous Gina down. Lily had a feeling she might have to fight for her man. But right now she didn't want to fight. She only wanted to be alone with Phillip. She could hardly wait for the party to end.

"Camille is ready to perform her last song, Lily," Phillip said urging her toward the two empty seats in front of the bandstand.

Lily was so engrossed in listening to Camille play she almost forgot the reasons why she resented Gina Frazier. When the music stopped, she glanced at Phillip. Just looking at him made her insides quiver. Although she'd been fighting her feelings for him since they met, she realized that she was losing the battle. She found that she craved his touch. She wanted—no needed him as much as she needed her next breath of life giving air.

The look of desire in her eyes made the male part of Phillip's anatomy harden in arousal. He never knew he could want any woman as badly as he wanted her. Seeing Gina again had stirred only his contempt. He glanced at the remaining guests and wished they'd go home. He was eager to have a private party with the guest of honor.

Phillip took Lily's hand and rubbed the center of her palm with his thumb and gazed deeply into her eyes, communicating his desire for her.

Lily's pulse quickened and she wanted more than anything to leave the party and take Phillip to her bed.

From across the room Suzette sat on the couch observing Phillip and Lily.

"Don't do it, Suzette," Kyle warned from his seat next to her.

"Don't do what?"

"You know what. Let it alone."

"Let it alone? You can't expect me to just stand by and do nothing while my son ruins his life."

"When Phillip and I talked a few days ago about the report you had me compile on Lily, he let me know in no uncertain terms that he wouldn't stand for any interference in his relationship with her. If you don't back off you're going to lose him. Is that what you want?"

"You know it isn't."

"Then walk softly, Suze."

Phillip and Lily stood talking to Nicholas and Camille, who were the last guests to leave the party.

"Camille, why don't you and Nick bring Xavier and Solange over this Saturday and we'll have a family picnic."

"Are you sure you want to do that? You know what absolute terrors your niece and nephew can be," Camille quipped.

"Yes, I do. Believe it or not I enjoy watching you two with the children. I have to admit that I get a little envious. Like you, I hope to one day have it all."

"Oh, so you think we have it all, little brother?" Nicholas grinned.

"You know you do." Noticing that Lily was awfully quiet during the exchange, Phillip assumed that she was feeling left out of the conversation and put his arm around her shoulder and gave it a reassuring squeeze.

"Nicholas, I think it's time we left these two alone,"

Camille said flashing her brother-in-law and Lily a knowing smile. "About Saturday, I think the twins would enjoy an outing. We'll be here at say one o'clock?"

"Sounds good to me."

Phillip offered to walk Nicholas and Camille to their car, but they refused.

He turned to Lily. "You were definitely the bell of the ball tonight, my beautiful tiger Lily."

"Do you know what would round out my evening?"

"No. Give me a hint."

Lily wet her lips easing them into a sexy, provocative smile. "You don't need one."

Phillip's expression turned serious. "Are you saying what I think you are? You have to be sure it's what you really want, Lily."

"I am sure." She took his hand and tugged him in the direction of the French doors.

He was glad his mother had gone to her room. The last thing he wanted was for her to make a scene. He stopped walking and pulled Lily into his arms and kissed her. The taste of her was like ambrosia on his tongue. The more he tasted the more he wanted. He lifted her in his arms and carried her through the gardens to her room. Once inside Phillip lowered Lily's feet to the floor, stepped back and just stood gazing at her for a moment, completely entranced.

Cupping her face in his two hands, he lowered his head and tenderly kissed her lips, then moved to the shell of her ear.

Lily heard him whisper her name, then he returned his mouth to hers and slowly drank from the fountain of her lips like a parched man savoring the sweet taste of life-giving water, but still finding himself thirsting for more. The power of the kiss streamed through her, exciting her, making her feel like a whole woman again, exuberantly alive and pulsing with the pleasure of it, something she hadn't come close to experiencing with any other man.

Right now at this very moment he encompassed her entire world, reducing it to this room. His lips promised and demanded, stroked and caressed, took and gave. Hungrily, she drew him in, his touch, his taste, his scent.

Their mouths moved against each other with ever increasing passion until her blood was racing hotly through her veins.

Then he trailed hot kisses down her throat, while his hands roamed over her buttocks, squeezing and caressing.

"Oh, my beautiful tiger Lily," he groaned. "I want you so much."

"You can't want me half as much as I want you, Phillip."

"I don't think that's possible."

"I've been fighting my feelings for so long, when all I've really wanted to do was love you with every part of myself."

"Want no more, my love."

Phillip stroked and petted her breasts, watching them peak beneath the thin, silky cloth. Eager to see her naked, he reached behind her and pulled down the zipper on her dress, then slipped the garment off her body and watched it float to the floor and land in a pool around her feet. Next he lifted her filmy camisole from her body.

"My God, Lily." He immediately lowered his lips to a breast and laved a nipple with his tongue.

When he sucked it deep into his mouth, a moan escaped her lips and a tingling sensation jetted to the heart of her womanly core.

"Oh, Phillip."

He peeled her panties down past her hips and thighs and followed their descent to the floor. Then he dropped down on his knees and quickly removed her shoes.

She ran her fingers through his hair. "Now, it's my turn."

"Your turn?" he said in a dazed voice as he looked up at her.

"To undress you."

Grinning, he rose to his feet. "By all means, be my guest."

"Actually you're my guest since this is my room. But we won't quibble about that. Will we?"

"No. We won't."

Lily helped him out of his dinner jacket, then unbuttoned his shirt. The sensual heat emanating from his hard muscular chest singed her fingers. She pushed the shirt off his shoulders and admired his tight six-pack abs. When she heard his sharp intake of breath, she stroked his skin. And smiling, pulled the shirt out of his pants and tossed it on the floor. When he slipped his foot out of his shoe she said.

"No. Let me." Then she proceeded to finish the job, removing the other shoe and his socks. Then she unfastened his pants and sent them plummeting to his feet.

Phillip stepped out of the pool of clothing and brought his hands to the waistband of his briefs.

"Uh-uh, that's my business, but I want it to also be my pleasure." He moved his hands away.

When Lily brushed her fingers across the front of the soft cotton briefs, she felt his manhood harden and swell. She swiftly divested him of the encumbrance and caressed his hot silky-smooth male flesh.

"You keep that up I won't last ten seconds."

She stopped and let out a husky chuckle. "I definitely want you to last longer than that." She molded her naked body against his.

"Lily."

She kissed his lips and led him over to her bed and urged him to sit down. After doing so he pulled her down on his lap and then wrapped his arms around her waist and starting from her stomach, he kissed a path of fire to her breasts and worshiped one nipple then the other.

The erotic play of his mouth on her ultra-sensitive globes was driving her crazy.

"Stop! Oh, please stop! You're torturing me."

"Only with pleasure, my tiger Lily. And it's only the beginning." Without further adieu he lifted, then, straddled her across his lap, deeply embedding himself firmly to the hilt inside her. Her gasp of surprised pleasure made his shaft throb and harden even more.

He swung his legs up onto the bed. "Ride me, Lily," he commanded.

Lily moved experimentally at first until she found a rapturous rhythm and settled into an addictive gliding motion. She quickened the pace, when he had learned it and started levering his hips upwards, as she came down. It had been a long time since she'd made love and she couldn't hold back. Her cries of sheer bliss seemed to go on and on, mounting and mounting, as spasm after ecstatic spasm shuddered through her femininity. A sudden explosive climax convulsed her body and she collapsed on top of him.

"I'm so sorry," she said moments later when she could catch her breath. "I don't know what came over me."

"It's all right, Lily. We've only just begun as the song goes."

"But you didn't—"

"This first time was just for you. We have all night to find rapture together. And believe me, I intend to make this a night neither one of us will ever forget."

Lily had to admit that she could hardly wait for the next episode to commence. Never before had she made love with such complete abandon.

Phillip reversed their positions, his hard male strength still deeply lodged in her pulsing sheath. He drew her legs around his hips and they began that age-old dance, her body rising and his falling to the intimate beat of love.

"Yes, yes, oh, yes," Lily chanted.

Phillip delved deeper, moving faster, building the friction, driving the heat up a notch, then another and still another. When he heard her cry out as she reached for that seemingly unreachable pinnacle of pleasure, he let his breath go with a sound that was part sigh, part groan and joined her in a mind-altering leap into a shattering vortex of pure sensation.

As Phillip lay gazing into Lily's sleep-relaxed face, his mind replayed each incredible session of rapture they'd shared all through the night. He felt a pang of guilt for continually waking her to make love with him. It was almost dawn, but he wanted her again. He couldn't seem to help himself. It was as though he could never get enough of her. An eternity wouldn't be nearly long enough.

Lily moaned softly as she slowly awoke. At the touch of questing fingers on the petals of her womanhood, the lingering languor from Phillip's lovemaking sprang into arousing titillating life.

"Phillip, I–" Her breath caught in her throat when he delved into the center of her flower. She opened to him and closed her eyes as he stroked her to the brink of release.

Then he quickly moved over her and extended her joy and reignited his own. And together they reached a plane that went beyond rapture.

CHAPTER NINETEEN

As she sat drinking her morning coffee, Suzette observed her son and Lily as they all ate breakfast out on the terrace. It didn't take a genius to figure out that the couple seated across from each other had spent an intimate night together. It was obvious in the looks that passed between them. They were barely aware of her presence. Lily Jordan was all wrong for Phillip. Why couldn't he see that? There had to be a way to stop them from making the biggest mistake of their lives.

"Nick and Camille will be bringing the twins over for a picnic on Saturday, mother."

Suzette smiled at her son. "It'll be good having them here."

"Why don't you invite Kyle?" Phillip's eyes narrowed when he saw the look in his mother's eyes. She and Kyle had obviously talked about what she had enlisted him to do, and Phillip's reaction to it. And she wasn't happy.

"All right. I'll ask him." Suzette wiped her mouth and dropped her napkin down on the table. "I have something I need to take care of. If you'll excuse me."

"Remember what I said, mother," he warned.

Suzette sent Lily a resentful look before going inside.

Lily sighed. The woman would never change her mind about her. She considered her good enough for her son to sleep with, but nothing more than that.

Phillip slid his hand over Lily's. "Don't look like that. Doesn't matter to me whether she approves or not. I want you in my life." He glanced at his watch. "I have to go to the hospital and check on a patient, but I'll be back as soon as I can." He rose from his chair and leaned over and kissed Lily. "I have a special day planned for you, Ms. Jordan."

She returned his kiss and smiled as she watched him go. She loved him so much, but there were other concerns besides his mother that they hadn't even touched on. Everything had happened so fast between them. Once they had thrashed out their differences, hang-ups and problems, then and only then would they have a chance at a future together.

"New Orleans is so full of history," Lily said, awed by her surroundings as they strolled through the Garden District, a section of the city she'd been dying to see.

"Then you like my surprise?"

"If I hadn't gone into modeling, I would have studied to be a history teacher. You probably find it hard to see me as that."

"Not at all. I sensed your interest in history when you told me the places you've been. You even thought my boring dissertation on the family history was interesting."

"I didn't consider it boring at all. It's a part of your heritage. A part of who you are."

Guilt pinched Phillip because he hadn't told her about the other important part of his heritage. He wanted her to open up to him and come to love him for himself. Had he waited too late?

"You're frowning."

"Oh, am I? You know author Anne Rice back-dropped her novels here in New Orleans."

"I read somewhere that she has a house in the Garden District."

"She does, but I doubt if she spends that much time there since its location has become public knowledge. I imagine she has hordes of fans dying to get her autograph." He laughed. "I guess I shouldn't have put it quite like that considering the subject matter of her books."

She laughed. "No, you shouldn't. You're priceless, doctor."

'You really think so?"

"Don't let it go to your head. Okay?"

"Are you hungry?"

"A little."

"You want to eat at Emeril's?"

"The bam, man?" She giggled.

"The very same."

After leaving Emeril's, Lily and Phillip found a spot along the banks of the Mississippi and sat enjoying a muffuletta from Central Grocery.

"Nick and I used to do this when we were children. We'd slip away from my mother's watchful eye and find our own fun."

"I bet she liked that."

"Ah, I wouldn't say that exactly. Look, we still have time to visit the Aquarium. Want to go?"

"Oh, yes."

It started to rain when they arrived and they quickly dashed inside and wondered from exhibit to exhibit.

Lily walked over to an underground tank. "The dolphins are awesome. Aren't they?"

"Yes, I agree they are."

"You aren't even looking at them."

"I've gotten sidetracked by a different kind of exhibit. You!"

"You're incorrigible, Phillip Cardoneaux."

"Not too incorrigible, I hope?" He whispered in her ear. "I, ah, know of a place where we can be completely alone."

Phillip traced a finger along Lily's hip as they lay in bed.

"This house belonged to my aunt. She left it to me. I rarely come here because of my heavy schedule at the hospital."

"I've wondered why that's so."

"Oh." He stopped stroking her.

"I know you're dedicated to your work, but is the reason spelled Gina Frazier?"

A muscle twitched in Phillip's jaw. "Partly," he answered. "I made my work my panacea after our relationship ended."

"And now"

"And now you have become my panacea." He kissed her lips and moved over her and eased himself inside her.

"Oh, Phillip," she moaned and wriggled her body beneath his and wrapped her legs around his hips.

He groaned, thrusting in and out over and over again, driving them both to a blissful completion.

"Oh, Lily, I love you so much."

"And I love you."

"Do you really?"

"If you have to question it, I need to show you more proof,"

"No, you don't. It's just that I've wanted this so much and wondered if it would ever happen. And now that it has—"

"Don't say anything else. Just savor what we have."

"I want to do more than that. I want to marry you, Lily."

"Not because we—"

"No. I want to live the rest of my life with you, have babies with you."

Lily froze. "I think we need to talk about that."

"What's wrong? Don't you want to marry me?"

"I do, but—"

"But what?" He eased his body off hers and lay beside her. "Is it because I'm white that you're unsure?"

"Well my parents are an interracial couple and—"

"We are not your parents."

"Maybe not, but I'm a product of their lust for each other. And I don't want any children of mine to have to go through what I did."

"It's the reason you were so resentful of Camille and my brother. That's not fair to us or them."

"It wasn't fair to me that my parents made my life a living hell."

"It doesn't have to be like that between us." He could tell that he wasn't making much progress in convincing her to the contrary. "I guess I should have told you the truth sooner."

She raised up on an elbow and looked at him. "What truth?"

"That I'm part black."

"But how–I don't understand."

"I didn't find out myself until a year ago. You see my maternal grandmother was only one quarter white and the rest black."

"Why didn't you tell me this before?"

"I wanted you to accept me as I am. When you told me you would-n't let yourself get involved with me because I was white it bothered me. My mother never told my father about herself for fear he would divorce her. As much as she claimed to love him, she never trusted him not to judge and condemn her."

"I see."

"Do you, Lily? I guess I'm more my mother's son than I realized. I seem to have inherited some of her tendencies."

"You should have told me before now."

"I know. Does it matter?"

"Not really? If we had children they'll probably have the same problems as I had to face."

"But the difference would be that we'd be there to help them."

"I don't want to take that chance, Phillip. If we get married, I don't want children."

Lily saw the expression on his face and her heart sank. They weren't going to be able to work it out. She'd seen him with his niece and nephew.

Phillip roiled it over in his mind. He wanted Lily, but he also want-ed children. In time he'd convince her to change her mind.

What if you can't, Cardoneaux? What then?

"In time you'll–"

"I think we'd better go."

"Don't shut me out, Lily. You said that you loved me."

"I do,"

"But not enough to have my children?"

Lily scrambled off the bed and started putting her clothes back on.

"I want children, but I love you more and I want to marry you. I know you've suffered because of your parents."

"I know you understand, but–"

He pulled her into his arms. "We belong together."

Lily snuggled against him. She wanted to be his wife, but having children was out of the question. Could he really accept that and not resent her later on down the road? She had a lot to think about. She should have felt relieved to find out he was part black, but she wasn't. He was more white than black and if they had children...

Why are you borrowing trouble, girl? You and Phillip don't get along like your parents.

But there was the possibility that they might later on. They were complete opposites who happened to attract. Her parents had been opposites too and look how they turned out.

You're letting your resentment of your parents cloud your judgment.

No. She wasn't. She wasn't. God, she was so confused.

Phillip saw the confusion and smiled in sympathy. If he could untangle it . . .

That's a pretty big if.

He loved her and he was willing to gamble that in time he could change her mind.

Or wear her down. What if you're wrong?

He'd worry about that shaky bridge before he had to cross it.

CHAPTER TWENTY

Lily stood on the dock at Magnolia Grove peering out over the Mississippi river. Right now its waters were so calm and serene, but during a storm it could turn treacherous, rage completely out of control, and flood its banks causing untold destruction. She wondered if in time Phillip had it in him to be as volatile.

At times her father had his serene moments. Before he and her mother had married they had probably thought they'd live happily ever after. What could have happened to change all that? What really baffled her was that they were still together?

You should talk to them about your feelings. It's something you've never done in the past. You've avoided them for the last five years.

She'd called them.

It's not the same thing and you know it.

How could seeing them possibly help her and Phillip?

No. This was something she'd have to work out for herself.

"Such heavy thinking, Lily pad."

"Carey."

"Yes. It's me, your friendly neighborhood photographer at your service."

"What are you doing here? I thought your next assignment was supposed to start today."

Carey walked over to her. "It was, but I've been reassigned to do a shoot in Spain this weekend instead. Mimi rescheduled the one in Italy for two weeks from today. Fabrizio Aggretti wants only you to model his new line." Despite her present mood, hearing him say that lifted her spirits."

"And besides, he prefers Dena DeLucia to do the shoot."

Dena was a pretty volatile, temperamental woman, but she was also an exceptionally talented fashion photographer.

"You don't mind?"

"It wouldn't do any good if I did, which I don't. Mimi respects my work, but sometimes she defers to the designer's preferences and whims. When I walked up just now you seemed to have the weight of the world on your shoulders, girlfriend."

"Phillip has asked me to marry him."

"So, what's your problem? You love him. Don't you? I know the man is besotted. Tell me why you're not happy as a clam?"

"I do love him, but he wants to have kids and I don't."

"Why? Don't tell me. It's because of your relationship with your parents. Isn't it?"

"I hear a lecture coming on."

"No. I'm not going to go there with you. You know how you feel, but–"

"Carey."

"So what are you going to do?"

"I don't know yet. After talking to Jolie and Henri and seeing how they handle things, I know mixed marriages can work, but I'm still leery about that happening for me and Phillip and any future kids we might have."

"What you want are guarantees. Life doesn't work that way. You have to take your chances like everybody else."

"The voice of wisdom has spoken."

"You're really messed up over this. Aren't you?"

"I don't want to talk about it anymore. Did Suzette give you a hard time when you arrived?"

"No. When I drove up, the Dragon Lady was getting into her car and she pretended not to see me. I consider that an improvement." Carey laughed. "The night of the party she acted like a straw and sucked it up when she had to be polite to me. She almost had me rolling, but I restrained myself. Just barely."

"You're terrible, Carey Graham. But you always make me feel better."

He grinned. "It's included in my job description. I thought you knew that?"

⸎

After Carey had gone, Lily sat on the Cardoneaux's private pier a while before returning to her room. For the last couple of days she'd seen very little of Phillip or his mother. She knew he was giving her space. But his patience was a kind of pressure. And so were his expectations of the future he wanted her to share with him. A future that included children.

That evening Phillip called to say he'd be late getting home from the hospital. Lily thought about having dinner in her room, but decided against it. She wasn't a coward. And besides, she wouldn't give Suzette the satisfaction of knowing that she'd gotten next to her.

"I didn't expect to see you this evening," Suzette said when Lily entered the dining room.

"You mean since Phillip won't be here. Right?" Lily waited until Edna had left after serving them to continue. "Phillip told me about your black heritage and why he only recently found out about it."

"That piece of information doesn't make you any more suitable for my son, Ms. Jordan. You're still not good enough for a man of his caliber."

"How is it that you feel justified to pass judgment on me?"

"You've no doubt done things in the past that could come home to roost if you marry Phillip. He's a dedicated doctor with a respectable reputation to uphold."

"Oh, so you think I'll tarnish his image by marrying him?"

"It could happen. Even if it doesn't, are you willing to give up your career to start a family. Having children is what Phillip has longed for most of his adult life. I can tell by your silence that you're not prepared to give him what he wants. If you love him as he thinks you do, or you say you do, you'll think long and hard about that."

Lily didn't have a comeback. Suzette was right: she did love Phillip enough to do what was best for him.

Phillip had been preoccupied all week: visions of Lily never more than a thought away. His future was so uncertain. Lily loved him. He didn't doubt that, but was it going to be enough?

"Hey, Phil. Phil?" Larry called to him.

"Larry, I'm sorry. What did you say?"

He frowned. "Is anything wrong?"

"No."

"I don't believe that for one minute. This is me, Larry. I know you, remember. Something is bothering you. Or is it a someone? You and Lily aren't having problems, are you?"

Phillip saw several nurses congregated at the Nurses' Station looking in their direction.

"Let's go to the lounge."

Once inside he said. "I want to marry Lily."

"But? I know there's one in there someplace?"

"I want children and she doesn't."

"Well, she is a model. Maybe when she's done modeling."

"It doesn't have anything to do with her career."

"Oh. Then maybe for some reason she can't have them."

"As far as I know, there's no physical reason why she can't. It has to do with the way she was raised and her hang-ups about mixed marriages. Evidently, she's suffered as a result of being raised by parents who constantly bickered and argued. I think she's afraid that things might turn out like that between us. I've tried to convince her that they won't, but—"

"She's afraid to risk it. Right? Maybe in time."

"That's what I'm counting on."

"I hope it all turns out right for you both."

"Thanks, man."

"Kyle is as bad as you and Nicholas when it comes to spoiling the children, Phillip," Camille commented as they sat enjoying glasses of lemonade at the picnic and watched Kyle Barnette and Suzette playing with Xavier and Solange. When he didn't smile, she frowned. "What's wrong? Is it Lily?"

"Yes, it is."

"I noticed the chill when I got here. At first I thought it was because of me. I know she doesn't care for me very much."

"I don't think it's you personally. It's what she's convinced herself that you represent."

"What exactly do I represent?"

"She sees you as some kind of abuser of children."

"She what!"

"Calm down. It's not what you think. You see, she was raised in a racially mixed household where her life was less than ideal to put it mildly. Her father is white and her mother is black and—"

"I understand now. Maybe I should have a talk with her."

"I don't know if it'll do any good. Jolie has tried to make her see that it doesn't necessarily follow that her children would suffer the way she did."

"I know how hard it is to separate yourself from childhood images. They sometimes feel as real now as they did in the past. If you let them they can become bigger than life."

"I learned that from what happened to my mother."

"You have to be understanding and sympathetic about her feelings, Phillip."

"I know."

Lily saw Phillip talking to his sister-in-law. Judging from the expression on his face they were discussing something heavy: probably the situation between her and

Phillip. Maybe his mother was right and she should get out of his life.

"My brother loves you," Nicholas said as he walked up. "Do you love him?"

"I'm not going to discuss it with you."

"I think we damn well *should* discuss it. I don't want to see him hurt."

"You think I would do that?"

"Maybe not intentionally. I just don't know. What I do know is that he's had more than his share of suffering, Lily. He loved Gina Frazier and she nearly destroyed him."

"Are you also speaking from personal experience? Did Camille make you suffer? Is she still making you suffer? And not just you, but your children?"

"We've had our share of problems. Who hasn't at one time or another. I can tell you this. Because of the unusual circumstances of our children's birth our relationship is unique. Camille and I know each other very well. We put our concern for the children first. Not everyone does. You don't think your parents did where you're concerned. Do you?"

Lily didn't get a chance to answer. Just then Camille and Phillip approached, each carrying a twin in their arms. Nicholas kissed her cheek and took Xavier from Phillip and they headed over to the small play yard set up beneath a near-by oak tree.

Phillip took Lily's hand. "I think we need to talk."

"Look, Phillip, I–"

"We're going to talk now."

Lily could see that there was no way she could get out of it. Phillip's features were set in that serious, determined expression she'd come to know so well. He tugged her in the direction of the gazebo overlooking the Mississippi. He opened the gate and waved for her to precede him inside.

Lily sat down on one of the cushioned seats lining the wall of the airy, latticed structure. Phillip sat down beside her.

"I'll be officially releasing you from my care in a matter of days. How much time do you think you'll need to decide whether you'll marry me?"

"Look, Phillip, I–"

"I know you have hang-ups about the past. I'm more than willing to help you sort them out. I'm a patient man and I love you so much. You know that."

Lily stood up and walked over to the gate, but didn't open it. She turned to face Phillip. "I love you too that's why I can't marry you. I know how much having children means to you. And it would be self-ish of me to stand in the way of your dream of being a father."

"But, Lily–"

"Don't say any more."

"I can't just let you walk out of my life. You've become a part of my very soul."

Tears trickled down her cheeks. "Phillip, please don't do this to me."

"We belong together, damn it. You know we do. I want children, but I want you more, my tiger Lily."

"You're saying that now, but what about later. You'll begin to hate me for wrecking your hopes and dreams. I won't do that to you. I won't."

"We can find a way, Lily."

"I've decided to leave tomorrow."

"Against your doctor's orders? You can't."

"My next modeling assignment begins next week." She wiped the tears from her face and opened the gazebo gate and headed back to the house.

Phillip wanted to go after her, but he decided that it wouldn't do any good right now. He wasn't giving up on her.

Somehow he'd convince her to change her mind about marrying him.

CHAPTER TWENTY-ONE

Phillip stood just inside the French doors of Lily's bedroom watching her sleep. Her hair was splayed across the pillow and she'd tossed the covers off. The moonlight shining on her body made it look like a marble statue. But the filmy champagne colored nightie offset that illusion because it revealed more than it covered of her oh so real body. And the part of her it revealed was a definite turn on. He shed his clothes and walked over to the bed and sat on the edge and bent over and kissed a dark pink nipple.

Lily whimpered, but didn't wake up. Phillip trailed a finger down to her waist. The nightie was hiked up over her hips, exposing the dark, blonde-brown patch of hair covering her womanhood. He groaned softly and delved a finger between the folds and caressed the sensitive pearl beyond. When he felt her quiver and moisten, then open to him, he removed his finger and slid his body over hers and slowly tunneled deep within her.

"Oh, Phillip," she moaned and started moving her hips in circular motions.

He kissed her deeply, delving his tongue in her mouth as his manhood imitated the same movements below.

"I love you, Lily. You can't leave me. You just can't."

He rode her deeply, plunging and retreating driving her out of her mind with pleasure over and over for what seemed like forever. One last thrust tossed them both over the summit.

"Phillip, you shouldn't have–"

"What? Made love to the woman I desire more than life itself? You ask too much of me, Lily. Listen, sweetheart. We don't have to have children. As long as I have you."

"Are you sure? Are you absolutely sure you can live with that?"

"Yes."

"Oh, my darling man, how I love you. I love you now more than ever for wanting to make that sacrifice for me."

Phillip made love to Lily all through the night. At the first light of dawn, he went back to his room to shave, shower and dress before going to the hospital. He couldn't let her go: she was his life. It wouldn't be much of one without her to share it with. Children were important, but not more important than his love for Lily.

Are you sure you can live with your sacrifice.

It's not a sacrifice.

Deep down are you still hoping to eventually change her mind? Be honest with yourself.

He was being honest. He was.

Lily was happier than she'd ever been in her life. She was going to marry the man she loved. He'd proved to her that he considered her more important than anything or anyone. When Edna brought her some croissants and juice for brunch, she told Lily that Phillip had instructed her not to wake her for breakfast, that he had to leave early for the hospital. It was almost lunchtime when she finished eating.

Lily showered and dressed and was about to go out when she heard a knock at the door. It opened before she could respond.

"At breakfast Phillip told me that you and he were getting married. You're a selfish little bitch, Lily Jordan, just like your mother. She ruined your father's life by marrying him."

"What are you talking about?"

"I've had your background investigated and the last report I received, the private detective had talked to one of your father's sisters. She told him that your father hadn't wanted children, and he told your mother he was contemplating having a vasectomy to insure it. And if she couldn't accept that he wouldn't marry her. She evidently wanted to have children and also your father so in order to have both she deliberately got pregnant."

"She couldn't possibly know that."

"Have you ever wondered why you never had sisters or brothers? According to your aunt, your father went ahead and had the vasectomy because he hadn't dared trust your mother not to get pregnant again." Suzette paused.

"Phillip wants children and you'll be denying him that chance if you marry him. His life could be rich and full, but for your selfishness. As long as you get what you want that's all that counts. Right? You'd marry him knowing what he would be giving up? Your mother purposely got pregnant knowing that your father didn't want children."

"Phillip and I love each other. My parent's situation was different."

"How do you know they didn't love each other, and because of what your mother did, the relationship changed to one of disagreement and mistrust. Do you want your relationship with Phillip to deteriorate into that?"

"I want you to leave right now, Mrs. Cardoneaux."

Suzette let out a disgusted sigh and left the room. Lily closed the door and slowly slid down it to the floor. She was the cause of her parents unhappiness. No wonder her aunt couldn't stand the sight of her. Because of her, her father had been trapped in the kind of marriage he never wanted. She couldn't, wouldn't do that to Phillip.

Lily rose from the floor and headed over to the closet and started pulling clothes out and tossing them on the bed. Tears began to well in her eyes, blinding her, and she sank into a chair and let them fall. If he were unhappy or unfulfilled, the only pleasure she and Phillip could ever find would be in each other's bodies. Like her parents had.

Her life with Phillip could deteriorate into that. His desire to have children would secretly burn inside him and eventually that desire would change to resentment and possible hatred. Nicholas was right. Phillip had suffered enough. She loved him and wouldn't allow him to suffer any more than he had already. In time he'd find a woman who wanted to have children with him. She could never be that woman.

It would be wrong to agree to have children just for his sake when she didn't really want them. What about the children?

Lily finished packing, wrote Phillip a letter, left it on her bed, then called a taxi.

Half an hour later as the taxi moved through the alley of trees toward the gate, Lily looked back. She'd come to love Magnolia Grove almost as much as she loved Phillip. And although leaving him broke her heart, she knew she'd made the right decision.

"You seem to be in good form this morning, doctor," Alice Clayborne commented as she entered the nurses' station and found Phillip whistling happily as he updated one of his patient's chart.

"I am, Alice. The woman I love has agreed to marry me."

One of her rare smiles broke out over her face and Phillip realized that Alice was a handsome woman.

"It's Lily Jordan, isn't it?"

"Yes, it is. She's the most beautiful girl in the world."

"I see you think so. Well, congratulations, Dr. Phil. I hope she realizes what a lucky woman she is."

"I'm the lucky one."

"So when's the wedding?"

"We haven't set a date yet."

"I know all the single nurses will be heartbroken."

"You're *all* heart, Alice." Phillip put the chart he was updating in the file rack and started down the hall.

"Phil."

He turned and smiled. "Larry. You can tell that matchmaking wife of yours to go out and buy herself a new dress."

Larry grinned. "You've ironed out all of your problems with Lily?"

"No. Not all, but we're getting there."

"But it's a go on getting married. I'm happy for you, man."

"I have a stop to make before heading home to Magnolia Grove and my woman."

Phillip practically floated out to the parking lot. His smile faded when he saw who the woman was leaning against his car.

"What do you want, Gina?"

"Now, is that any way to talk? We can start over, Phillip. Marrying Gerald was a mistake and I've corrected it."

"So? That doesn't mean I want you back. I told you that I'm in love with Lily. In a few weeks we'll be getting married."

"You hardly know the woman. Does she really understand you?"

Phillip laughed. "The way you do? Gina, please. It's been over for a long time. If you knew me like you claim you do, you'd know that what you did isn't something I can ever forgive. You walked out on me and went straight to Gerald. You weren't interested in being a doctor's wife."

"That was then. I've come to realize what a mistake I made. I should have–"

"It's too late, Gina."

"You think this international supermodel is what dreams are made of. Don't you? Believe me, she's no saint."

"And you are? Look, Gina, find yourself another man. What about Jack?"

"He's just a friend. There is nothing serious going on between us."

"I don't really care whether there is or not. I'm not interested. You have a nice life with someone else. I'm anxious to go home to Lily, so if you wouldn't mind."

She moved away from the door. "You're going to regret talking to me like that, Phillip. You wait until your precious Lily dumps you. You'll come crawling back to me. And I just might not take you back."

"Keep on dreaming, Gina."

Phillip watched her stalk angrily to her car and shook his head. The nerve of the woman.

He drove to Rothschild's Jewelry on Royal Street.

As he approached the door, he was met and escorted inside by one of the owners.

"Dr. Cardoneaux, we have the rings ready for you, sir. I must say that what you commissioned us to create is most unusual."

"The one I had you create them for is an unusual woman."

"I can tell you love her very much."

Phillip grinned. "Oh, how?"

"The aura of love surrounds you like a nimbus. Follow me to our private viewing room."

Anxious to see the ring, Phillip paced impatiently as he waited for

Mr. Rothschild to bring the tray to him.

He was speechless when he saw it. On a bed of cream colored velvet, the three carat tiger-eye amber stone engagement ring glittered with life and energy, mounted on its gold, tiger lily flower setting. The band was exquisitely designed in a tiger lily pattern. The pattern continued on the matching wedding band encrusted with five one carat amber topaz stones.

"I would say she was a fortunate young woman to be loved so deeply and so well."

"Believe me, Mr. Rothschild, I am the fortunate one."

When Phillip walked into the house, it seemed strangely quiet for some reason. His mother was probably having dinner with a friend at the country club. He hoped the friend was Kyle Barnette. He could be good for her. If she got involved with him she wouldn't have time to interfere in his life. And she would leave him and Lily alone. What was that he'd told Gina? To keep dreaming?

He headed for the guest suite instead of upstairs to his room. He didn't want to wait another minute to see the woman he loved and give her the engagement ring. He knocked on her door, and when there was no answer, he turned the knob.

"Lily, my love." He smiled while easing open the door. When he saw the envelope lying on the bed, his heart dropped to his feet. He picked it up and tore it open.

Phillip
You know how much I love you. That was
never in question. Because of that love
I have to let you go. It would be wrong
of me to make you give up your dream.
I know what you're going to say, that it
doesn't matter, but it does. I want
your happiness and the only way you'll
find it is with a woman who can give you

what I can't.
This is good bye, I will always love you
Lily

"No, Lily. I will never be happy without you." He lifted the gift box out of his jacket pocket and then sank down on the bed. The box slipped from his fingers and tumbled to the floor. Tears slowly trickled from his eyes and down his cheeks.

CHAPTER TWENTY-TWO

Phillip sat on a seat inside the gazebo staring out over the river. The pain he had felt since Lily left was gradually dulling into a never-ending agony, rotting away his very soul. God, he loved her so much, but his love had evidently not been enough to hold her.

It had been a week since she had gone and he was slowly losing his mind. He couldn't eat and wasn't sleeping. Alice had already threatened to go to the hospital administrator and demand that he be ordered not to work 24/7 as he had been doing.

"It won't work, Phil. Believe me, I know," Nicholas said opening the gate of the gazebo.

"What won't work, big brother?" He shot to his feet. "Driving myself until I drop so I'll be so tired I can fall asleep without dreaming about her, aching to feel her in my arms?"

Nicholas walked over to his brother and hugged him.

"Nick, I don't know how I'm going to get through this."

"I'll help you. I know what you're going through. I know what it's like to try with all your heart and still fail. Despite doing everything I could think of, Lauren divorced me. At the time I thought it was the end of the world. Then I met Camille and knew that I hadn't loved Lauren as much as I thought. Maybe Lily isn't the right woman for you and—"

"Don't say it." He pulled away from Nicholas. "Do you really think I could love another woman the way I love Lily? She loves me, Nick, as much as I love her. I know that. I was so sure I had convinced her that we didn't have to have children. That we could be happy just the two of us."

"Phil. Remember when we thought that Xavier might not be my son. I made myself believe that if we didn't have the DNA tests, I could live with it. I was in denial. I realized after it was confirmed that he was my son, that I had been fooling myself. I wouldn't have been able to live with it.

"You know what to expect from Lily. She's made it clear that she doesn't want children. Knowing you as I do, I know you were gambling that you'd be able to change her mind."

"I could have. I know I could have, in time."

"What are you going to do now? You can't go on like this."

"I think you had better go home, Nick. I'll work through this by myself."

"If you need to talk–"

"I know where to find you."

"I hate seeing you suffer like this. I thought all the pain was behind you when you and Gina broke up."

"So did I."

"You have to look like you enjoy wearing Signore Fabrizio's designs, Lily. Let us do it one more time, eh?"

Lily glared at Dena DeLucia. The Italian woman may be a genius behind the camera, but she was also a merciless slave driver.

"Turn to the left. Not like that. *Dios mio*. You are moving your arms and legs like a rubber band tied to sticks. There is no fluidity in you. What is the matter with you?"

"I have a headache."

Dena threw up her hands. "*Scusi mio*. Always the headache. Yesterday it is the headache. Today it is the headache. You take the pain killer, yes?"

"I did, but–"

"*Basta*! We stop for this day. Go! You are no good for this." She shook her head. "I do not know why Signore Fabrizio want only you for the shoot."

"Maybe because I'm right for it," Lily said simply and walked out of the studio and took a taxi to the apartment Mimi had sublet for her use during her stay in Rome. She really did have a headache, but no headache remedy created could take away the pain of losing Phillip.

You didn't lose him. You threw him away.

The ache in her heart was almost more than she could bear, knowing that it was all too true. At night she lay awake thinking about him. When she did manage to sleep she'd dreamt about him. The dreams were so vivid she had woken up, moaning, her femininity hot and quivering with unsatisfied desire.

But she wouldn't give in and call Phillip. It was best that she learn to forget him and he to forget her.

As if that's going to happen in this lifetime. You and Phillip belong together, girl.

She couldn't give him what he really wanted.

But you can.

No, she couldn't. She'd never be enough for him.

The next morning she called Dena DeLucia's studio and was told that she wouldn't be needed today. She'd counted on being busy to keep her mind off Phillip. What would she do with herself? Sightseeing wasn't very much fun when you went alone. Several men she'd met wanted her to go out with them, but she couldn't bring herself to accept their invitations. She felt as though she were being disloyal to Phillip.

She decided to go shopping on the *Via Veneto*. After an hour she walked to a *trattoria* near the Spanish Steps. A couple who were obviously in love sat at a table across from hers holding hands and staring adoringly at each other. Tears welled in Lily's eyes. They could be she and Phillip. She had to stop torturing herself like this. Maybe when Giovanni called as she knew he would, she'd go out with him. She'd make herself forget Phillip.

"Phillip, you have to stop driving yourself like this," Suzette chided at the breakfast table.

"Don't nag, Mother."

"What are you trying to do? Work yourself to death? It's time you concentrated on finding the right woman."

"Lily is the right woman. You think because she's gone
I can just turn my love off and on like a light switch? I
I love her, Mother."

"Even after what she's done?"

Phillip shot up from his chair and tossed his napkin on the table.
"I'm not going to discuss Lily with you. I won't be home for dinner
tonight."

"Are you working late again?"

"No. I'm having dinner with Henri and Jolie."

"At least you're getting out. You'll meet someone who will want to
share every facet of your life. Give yourself a chance."

"You just don't understand. Do you?"

Phillip strode through the garden to his car. Why couldn't his
mother leave him the hell alone. It was hard enough living without
Lily, but for his mother to keep mentioning going out with someone
else was driving him crazy. There was no one else for him, but Lily. If
he couldn't have her, he didn't want anyone else. Maybe he should
move into the house he'd inherited from his aunt for a while.

"I beat you again. You're no competition at all this evening, Phil,"
Henri complained in disgust as he started putting away the backgammon set.

"Maybe you're just getting too good for me that's all, Henri," he
said looking out over the Quarter from the Puissant's balcony.

"That's bull."

Jolie brought them bottles of beer. When Phillip just looked at it
and made no move to drink it, she frowned.

"I know it's hard for you, but–"

"Don't, Jolie. I can't handle it right now. Just be my friend."

"I'll always be that. I'm worried about you, Phillip. You've lost
weight and you have a haunted look about you. Aren't you sleeping at
all?"

"Not really. No matter how hard I try, I can't stop thinking about her."

"It'll get better, Phil," Henri said sagely, squeezing his shoulder. "Love is often a pretty rocky road to travel. Your life will smooth out eventually."

"If I'm depressing you two, I can leave. The last thing I want to do is bring anybody down."

"Don't be silly. Of course you're not depressing us. We thought we were succeeding in cheering you up."

"Lily is the only one who will ever make that happen. And right now she's in the city of romance, probably with some smooth-talking Italian wining and dining her."

"You can always go after her, Phillip," Jolie suggested.

"She doesn't want to be a part of my life. I thought after I'd told her that we didn't have to have children, she would marry me. She agreed, then the next thing I knew she'd changed her mind. Something must have happened, but what?"

"You weren't being completely honest with her and maybe she realized it. I'm convinced that she loves you as much as you love her. Maybe once she's had time to think things over she'll come back to you."

"I wish. But I doubt it." He rose from his chair. "I'd better go. I'll be staying in my aunt's old house, a few blocks from here, for the next few days. I need some space. And I know I definitely won't get it if I go back to Magnolia Grove. My dear mother will make sure of that."

Jolie hugged him. "You take care, Phillip. We love you. If you need us to do anything for you just ask. Okay?"

He smiled sadly at her. "Okay."

After reaching his aunt's house, the minute he entered the bedroom, he thought about the last time he had been here. He and Lily had made love is this very bed. God, would the pain ever stop. He couldn't bring himself to sleep in it. He went down the hall to the guest room.

BEYOND THE RAPTURE

Lily's evening out was a mistake. She knew it when Giovanni arrived to pick her up. When she opened the door, standing in the shadows with the light shining on his black curly hair, he looked like Phillip. She almost called him that, but managed to stop herself in time. They ate dinner at *La Pergola*. The special of the house was fried zucchini flowers with seafood consommé, caviar, and saffron. It was delicious, but it might as well have been ashes for all the enjoyment she'd gotten.

"What is it, *carissima*?" Giovanni lifted her hand to his lips. "Is the food not *deliciosa*?"

"It's very delicious."

"Si. Then it must be the *campania*?"

"It's not you, Giovanni. You've been wonderful."

"But I'm not the man you want to be with, no?"

"No. I mean yes. I'm sorry for spoiling your evening."

"You are not doing that, *carissima*. You are in love, but not with me. Can you not go to him, and as you Americans say, 'fix up?'"

Lily smiled. "Make up, Giovanni. I'm afraid not."

"Do you wish me to take you back to your apartment?"

"No. Take me dancing. I know it will make me feel better."

His expression said he didn't believe it would, but he took her to several *testaccios*, night clubs, on the *Via Galvani*. Giovanni was the perfect date all evening.

Still she was miserable.

It was no use, she wanted the man she loved to do the city with her. She wanted Phillip.

CHAPTER TWENTY-THREE

"I think you have had enough of our new vintage, Phillip," Armand scolded, taking the half-empty wine glass from his fingers.

"You're right. Can't drown my sorrows. There are not that many bottles of wine in the world. I'm going back to the house."

Armand shot him a sympathetic smile. "Amour, she can be very painful. Believe me, I know."

Phillip laughed. "I guess everyone knows about me and Lily."

"Why don't you go to Italy and convince her to come back with you."

"It's not that simple, Armand."

"Yes. It is."

"You don't understand."

"I understand only too well. I would be happily married to Michelle if I had done what I'm telling you to do. She was an artist and wanted to study in Paris. I told her my place was here in New Orleans and if she loved me she would stay here and study at Tulane. We argued and she flew to Paris. I was a proud fool and let her go, thinking she would give in and come back to me. If I'd been smart I would have gone to Paris to be with her. I had no ties here. By the time I came to my senses and went after her, she'd met and married a fellow artist and left Paris. I never did find out where she went. It wouldn't have mattered anyway. The point is that I don't want you to have any "if I could've, would've, should've.""

"I appreciate you telling me this, Armand, but I can't follow your advice."

Phillip left the vineyard and mounted his horse and headed back to the house, but when he reached the path leading to the stable, he changed his mind and went in the opposite direction. He rode to the place where he and Lily had gone on their picnic. He dismounted, then walked his horse over to the tree that had shaded them while they ate. The ache in his heart was almost unbearable. As he started to climb back into the saddle, a rider approached. He frowned when he recognized who it was.

"I've been waiting for the opportunity to talk to you,

Phillip," Gina said with a triumphant smile as she slid from her saddle to the ground.

"I can't imagine why."

"Don't be rude, darling. It doesn't become you. You're well rid of Lily Jordan. She was all wrong for you."

"Look, Gina."

"Give me another chance to make you happy, Phillip.

I've changed. We could have that family you've always wanted and can never have with Lily."

Phillip stared at her. "What did you say?"

"I'm asking you to take me back so we can—"

"No, not that. I want to know where you came up with that idea about Lily."

"Everyone knows that."

He grabbed her by her forearms. "No, they don't. I want to know how you found that out? And I want to know *now*."

"You're hurting me."

"I'll do more than that if you don't tell me what I want to know."

"You've been drinking."

"Not nearly enough. Give, Gina."

She jerked out of his hold and rubbed her arms.

"All right. You were never like this before. What has happened to you?"

"Tell me, Gina or so help me I'll—"

"All right. I was at the country club the other day and I overheard your mother talking to Kyle Barnette. She told him that she was glad she'd hired an investigator to delve deeper into Lily's background. She was telling Kyle that her little talk with the woman had made her see the light. If Lily doesn't want to have your children, Phillip, I—"

"No. You can't ever take her place. I'd rather be married to Lily and remain childless than to have any children with you. I don't love you,

Gina. You destroyed whatever feelings I had for you when you left me and went to the arms of another man. I wasn't what you wanted then and you're not what I want now. You got that? Accept it."

Phillip climbed into the saddle and rode back to the house as fast as he could. If she'd done what he thought she had, his mother–he didn't dare finish the thought. It was too horrific to consider. He stormed into the house.

"Mother! Where are you?"

"Phillip, what's the matter?" she said entering the living room from the terrace.

"You know damn well what! How could you? You know how much I love Lily."

"What are you raving about?"

"Sit down, Mother." When she hesitated. "I said sit down!"

"How dare you speak to me like that."

"You're lucky I don't break your neck. I told you–no, I warned you not to interfere, but you took it upon yourself to go against my wishes. Don't look so surprised. Gina overheard a conversation between you and Kyle at the country club."

Suzette had the grace to guiltily look away.

"I did it for your own good. You're better off without that–"

"Don't say another word, Mother! Please, don't." He staggered a little unsteadily over to the couch across from her and dropped into it. He forced himself to calm down.

"What did you tell Lily?"

"I told her what I'd found out about her family. She did the right thing in leaving. She could never have made you happy."

"What exactly did you tell her, Mother?" he demanded impatiently.

"That her father never wanted children and her mother trapped him into marriage by getting pregnant."

"I won't ask where you got the information. Do you know what you've done, Mother?"

"I've prevented you from entering into a childless marriage to the wrong woman."

"The way you say that is almost fanatical."

"I'm not a fanatic. I love you."

He laughed humorlessly. "You drive away the woman I love and you tell me you love me. Your idea and mine on the subject differs drastically."

Phillip pushed up from the couch to his feet and started to leave the room.

"What are you going to do?" Suzette asked anxiously.

"Guess?"

"You can't mean to go after that–that woman!"

"You must be psychic, Mother, because that is exactly what I'm going to do."

"But you can't."

"Oh, can't I? Don't push it. I'm mad as hell at you right now. But I'm restraining myself because you're my mother."

"Phillip, I–"

"Not another word. I now understand exactly how Nicholas felt when you tried to break him and Camille up. You know what, Mother? You're a control freak. You have to have everything your own way. And I see that you're never going to change. I'll tell you one thing. If you don't accept Lily, you won't be seeing me at all because I'll leave this house. And I won't be coming back."

"You can't leave this is your house, your legacy."

"None of it holds any meaning for me without Lily. If you'll excuse me, I'm going up stairs and shower, then I'm going to call the hospital and get time off. I'll be booking a flight on the next plane to Rome. While I'm gone, I want you to think about what I've said because I mean every word."

"*Dios mio*," Dena DeLucia screeched. "You are supposed to be enjoying wearing these designs. Instead you act like you can not wait to get out of them."

As much as Lily hated to admit it, the woman was right. She had to snap out of her funk and do her job. She turned up the wattage on her smile.

"Better. Now turn to the left. Yes. That is it. Move over to the *Fontana* and run your fingers through the water. Put joy into your expression."

All Lily could think of was that she'd left the most important part of her life in New Orleans. Any other time being here in Roma would be so exciting. *Fontana delle Tararughe in Piazza Mattei* had stood since 1581. It's Renaissance history would have fascinated her at another time, but not now. None of the beautiful scenery around her at any of the other shooting locations she modeled in had interested her either.

Giovanni came along to offer suggestions to Dena and lend Lily moral support. He was head designer for Fabrizios.

"Dena, take it easy on Lily."

"I am the photographer Fabrizio chose. Me, Dena DeLucia. *Scusi mio, per favore*. Let me do my work without interference.

Giovanni smiled and glanced at his watch. "It is time for siesta."

Dena glared at him and started folding up her equipment.

Lily laughed at the exchange. It seemed that Dena had met her match.

"You really shouldn't have done that, Giovanni."

"Yes. I should. That woman is a terror. Come, we will have lunch. I have brought a basket filled with wonderful things."

Lily sighed. Giovanni was handsome, thoughtful and an all-around nice guy, but he wasn't Phillip. But then no man was.

"You go away in your mind. Come back, Lily. We walk across the *Piazza* to the park and we eat. Yes?"

"All right."

As they ate, they observed small children playing and running and their parents chasing after them, with the older ones laughing and teasing and making complete nuisances of themselves.

A blanket of sadness descended on Lily. This was what Phillip wanted: children to enrich his life. Why couldn't she be what he wanted her to be? Why couldn't she give him what he wanted?

Lily and Giovanni returned to the *Fontana*, and he waited while she finished the day's shoot, then drove her back to her apartment.

"My assignment in Rome is almost done, Giovanni."

"When it is, we can spend more time together. You don't have to be in London for a few days."

"Look, Giovanni, I don't think–"

He drew her into his arms. "Do not think, *carissima*," he said and then kissed her.

He was a good kisser, but she didn't feel any of the fireworks or experience Roman candles going off as she did when Phillip had kissed her. She laughed at her unintentional play on words. She was in Rome, but romance didn't enter into it. She would only ever love one man.

She pushed against Giovanni's chest. "Please."

"All right, Lily. If you want to go out later, call me.
You have the number to my cell. Yes?"

"I do," Lily said as she walked him to the door.

"If you want to forget about this man, you must replace him with another, eh?"

Lily opened the door. "I'll see you around, Giovanni."

He bent to kiss her, but she turned her face away and it landed on her cheek.

"*Ciao, carissima.*"

She closed the door and leaned against it and started crying.

"Phillip, oh, Phillip. I love you. I need you so much."

CHAPTER TWENTY-FOUR

Lily was glad the assignment had finally ended. She would rest here for a few days before flying to London for the next shoot. She'd be meeting Carey there. He would be a welcomed change from Dena DeLucia. She had to laugh. Carey would appreciate hearing that.

She entered her apartment and went to the bathroom to shower. She turned on the water and while it was heating, she took off her clothes. There was a knock at the door.

Now, who could that be. It couldn't be Giovanni, they'd said their good byes. Fabrizio had promised to send her one of the swim wear outfits she'd modeled that she liked. She turned off the water and pulled on a robe and then opened the door.

"I couldn't let you go, my tiger Lily."

"Oh, Phillip," she cried, launching herself into his arms. "Baby, how did you find me?"

"Mimi. I convinced her that it was a matter of life and death that I find you."

"Is that the truth?"

"You know it is. I love you, Lily." He picked up his suitcase and set it down just inside the doorway and then pushed the door closed with his foot.

"If–" Lily began.

Phillip stopped the flow of her words with a kiss and undid the tie on her robe and slid the garment off her shoulders and moved his lips to her throat and caressed her breasts. He felt her body shudder with desire beneath his fingers.

"God, Lily, I've missed you so much. You have no idea how much I've suffered."

"Oh, yes, I do. I've been burning in a private hell of my own."

"It stops right now." He lifted her in his arms and carried her into the bedroom and lowered her onto the bed. Then he stepped back and quickly shed his clothes and climbed in beside her.

Raised on an elbow, he gazed lovingly into her eyes and stroked her face.

"All I want to do is shower you with love, my beautiful tiger Lily."

"But what about—"

He placed a finger across her lips. "You mean everything to me. My life isn't worth living without you. If you don't want to have children so be it. I'll have you."

"Will I be enough? Your mother—"

"Forget about what she said. I'd never trap you in a relationship like your parents had or subject any children to what you endured. I had hoped that in time you would change your mind, but I now know that's not going to happen."

"But can you live with that?"

"Yes. I can't imagine life without you. Haven't I told you that you're my panacea."

She smiled. "Yes, you have." She slid her body over his, taking him inside her to the hilt. Phillip groaned at the hot delicious slide into pure ecstasy.

"Lily," he gasped, on a hoarse sigh as he automatically clamped his hands on her hips to hold her tightly over him and then reversed their positions. He surged deeply, withdrew slowly, letting her feel every shift of muscle and tissue, then he plunged again, watching her eyes lose focus, drugged with pleasure.

"Phillip," she whimpered. "What are you doing to me?"

"I'm showering you with my love," he answered lowering his voice to a husky velvet growl.

Every time he moved, he caressed the sensitively aroused walls of her femininity, repeatedly showering her body with rapture. It went beyond rapture.

His mouth covered hers, equally showering it with bliss. He brushed her breasts with the light matting of chest hair as he moved against her, shaping their bodies into an intricate sculpture. But they were far from being cold marble statues. Instead passion had transformed them into inspired, animated performers in love's ancient dance.

Lily was the epitome of every fantasy he'd ever dreamed of, and he'd almost lost her. He wanted to possess her body and soul. She was his. When she lifted her hips, he surged deeply into her. She cried out and at the moment her climax started convulsing her body, his own body shook violently and they came together.

The haze of lovemaking slowly cleared.

"Oh, God, Lily."

"What's wrong?"

"I got carried away and didn't use protection."

"Don't worry about it. It's not the right time of the month."

"Are you sure? I don't want to do anything to hurt you. The last thing I want to do is trap you into marriage the..."

"The way my mother did my father," she finished. "I know you wouldn't do anything like that. Above all else I trust you completely about that. I love you, Phillip."

"Will you marry me?"

She hugged him and kissed his lips. "Yes, I will." She urged him to cover her, but he eased away and reached for his pants.

"You say it's a remote possibility, but I'm not taking any more chances. In the future we'll need to go on some kind of contraceptive regimen." He moved over Lily and sank into her and he closed his eyes at the exquisite pleasure he experienced reconnecting to her.

Jet lag took over after they'd made love for the third time, and Phillip fell asleep still joined to Lily.

Later Lily awoke to a heavy weight on top of her and a hardening, pulsing sensation sheathed deep inside her femininity. She smiled coming wide awake. Realizing the man she loved was awake, aroused and ready, she moved her hips in circular motions against him. The action ignited flames that quickly burst into a passionate fire that consumed them totally.

"Talk about a wake up call," Phillip growled, encompassing her in his embrace.

"I kind of liked it too." Lily eased out of his arms and off the bed. "Don't worry I'm not leaving you. Let's shower together, then I want us to visit some of the romantic places in Rome."

"I didn't come all this way to go sightseeing unless the sights are you and I get an exclusive tour." He reached out and fondled her breast.

She moved back a step. "Since I arrived in Rome, day after day, I've watched lovers enjoying each other's company. I was jealous and envious."

Phillip smiled tenderly. "You were?"

"Yes."

"And no sweet-talking Italian has tempted you to go out with them?"

"There were a few, and I did go out with one of them, but he wasn't you. I realized I only wanted to go out on the town with the man I loved."

In that case we'd better take that shower so we can get started."

"I'm glad you've been here before and understand

Italian," Phillip remarked as Lily instructed the taxi driver where to take them.

"I know only a few key phrases here and there, and how to order food. Giovanni helped me with the rest."

Phillip's eyes narrowed. "Who is this Giovanni?"

"He's Fabrizio's lead designer."

"And?"

Lily smiled. "Are you jealous?"

"Do I have reason to be?"

"You really are jealous."

"Of any man who spends time with my woman."

"I love hearing you call me that." Lily kissed him lingeringly on the lips. "You have nothing to worry about, doctor. You're the only medicine I'll ever need."

"Where are we going by the way?"

"*Montevecchio a trattoria* hidden in a square near *Piazza Navona*, in the heart of ancient Rome. It's also where artists Raphael and Bramante had studios. It's said that Lucrezia Borgia was a frequent visitor to both."

Phillip grinned. "You really should have been a history professor. Beauty and brains, what a dynamite combination. And I get them both in a unbelievably sexy wrapping. What a lucky man I am."

"Sexy wrapping, huh?"

"Don't go prickly on me, cactus Lily. I'm the only one who will ever after have the pleasure of unwrapping you."

They got out of the taxi and Lily handed the driver a few lira. Hand in hand she and Phillip entered the little restaurant. A waiter immediately walked up and escorted them to a table near the front window.

"We'll have the roebuck with polenta. And the house vino," she ordered in Italian."

"Very impressive, Signorina Jordan," Phillip quipped.

"Flattery will definitely get you somewhere, doctor."

"Not where I would like to be at this very moment." Phillip grumbled. "This is going to be a long day."

"Are you by any chance looking forward to tonight?"

"You have no idea how much. It's all I can do to keep my hands off you, tiger Lily."

"Then it's true that absence makes the heart grow fonder?"

"More like abstinence makes the body randier."

Lily punched him on the arm. "You're bad.

"Not as bad as I would like to be if given the opportunity."

"Poor baby. It's only been an hour since we made love.

I never knew you could be so much fun."

"I'm not usually. Gina used to say I could be down right boring at times." He smiled at her. "You bring out all my more interesting attributes."

She took his hand in hers and gazed into his eyes.

"I love you with all my heart."

A wandering violin player entered the little restaurant. Phillip signaled him over to the table.

"Ask him to play some romantic songs, Lily."

She used a combination of sign language, body language and Italian words to convey what they wanted him to play. When she handed him money, he grinned and said.

"*Grazie, Signorina, grazie.*" And he kissed her hand.

"You've made another conquest."

"He was just being typically Italian."

They enjoyed the music and danced the afternoon away on the tiny dance floor.

"We've been here so long they're going to ask us to leave."

"They would never be so rude."

The waiter brought them a complimentary bottle of champagne. A distinguished older man followed him smiling.

Lily spoke to him in Italian.

Phillip looked puzzled. "We didn't order this."

"The man I was talking to happens to be the owner and he sent it to our table because he has a soft spot in his heart for lovers."

"It's obvious to everyone that we belong together."

"Everyone but your mother."

"That's because she doesn't want to acknowledge it. When we return to Magnolia Grove I can almost guarantee that her attitude will have undergone a surprising sea change."

"Did you threaten her?"

"Let's just say that I made her a promise."

"About my going back with you."

"Didn't Mimi call you? After I told her it was a life and death situation, she said that you didn't have to go to London and that Simone would fill in for you." He frowned at the look on Lily's face. "You're not upset about that. Are you?"

Any other time she would have been because she knew how anxious Simone was to replace her, but not now. Phillip was her complete focus.

"No. I'm not upset. How much time do you have before you have to get back to the hospital?"

"I took an indefinite leave of absence. I wasn't sure how much time

I'd need to convince a certain lady that she couldn't live without me."

"It didn't take long. As you soon found out I was easy."

"Not hardly. So where are we going next?"

They walked from fountain to fountain, starting with *Bernini*'s fountain in the *Piazza Navona*, then on to *Trevi* Fountain where of course they tossed in a coin to ensure their return to Rome. Their favorite was the fountain *Bernini* created at *Piazza Barberini*, *Fontana del Tritone*, a magnificent work of art. Lily related that it had been standing since 1642. It revealed the sea god blowing through a shell.

"Isn't it wonderful, Phillip," Lily remarked when they arrived by *carazzi*, in front of the Forum. "It looks so romantic bathed in moonlight."

"I agree. In fact it inspires me."

"Oh, to do what?"

"Use your imagination, tiger Lily."

"Are you trying to tell me that you're, ah, ready to go back to my apartment and fool around?"

"I won't be fooling. I intend to be explicitly serious about our love-making."

He caressed her lips. "We can paint the town tomorrow night."

"Because you want to scorch the bed tonight."

"I told you, beauty and brains wrapped in a sexy package: pure dynamite."

"In that case, I think we should go and explode together."

"I'm all for it."

"I'm going to need a doctor if we don't slow down," Phillip quipped.

"Weren't you the one–"

"Who wanted to scorch the bed? The very same, but I didn't mean that we should try to burn it to ashes."

"Are you complaining?"

"No. I'm too busy enjoying," he groaned thrusting deeper.

Lily murmured words of love over and over again.

Moments later, they soared to the heavens, reaching for euphoric oblivion and succeeding utterly.

Morning arrived finding the lovers still blissfully entwined. Phillip was the first to awaken. He smiled, admiring Lily's lush golden body. He would have loved to have had a daughter who looked just like her.

"Regrets, Phillip?"

"No, my darling tiger Lily. I want to make you my wife."

"When do you want to get married?"

"We can do it here in Rome." He brought out the gift box. "I have your rings. Hold out your left hand," he commanded.

Lily did as he said and Phillip slipped the engagement ring on the third finger.

"Oh, it's absolutely beautiful."

"See, I even brought its mate. We can get married here."

"Making our marriage a *fait accompli*? I don't think so. Your mother already doesn't trust me. What will she think?"

"I don't really care what she thinks, but I do care what you think. We'll wait and have a big wedding at Magnolia Grove if that's what you want."

"Not a big wedding, just a modest one at Magnolia Grove in say six weeks?"

"You got it. In the meantime I think we should work on perfecting our honeymoon skills."

"Practice makes perfect, huh?"

"I told you beauty and—"

"If you say it one more time I'm going to—"

"What? Love me to death."

"You're impossible."

"I am when I'm with you."

"What about breakfast?"

"Let's make it brunch," he said drawing her on top of him.

Needless to say they picked up where they left off after brunch.

"Do we have to go out?" he groused.

"Now, Phillip," Lily chided. "We're flying to New Orleans tomorrow."

"Oh, all right. I can't seem to get enough of you, sweet woman."

"Or I you, you gorgeous hunk of man. But we'll have a lifetime to try."

"This place is unbelievable. There has to be over 500 labels of wine," Phillip commented as they waited for their food to arrive.

"Lily?" came a deep throaty male voice.

"Kenton!" she choked out.

He raked an appreciative glance over her body. "How long have you been in Rome?"

Phillip cleared his throat. "Lily?"

"Ah, Kenton Davies, Phillip Cardoneaux."

Kenton extended his hand. "Former meets latter, I presume."

"Former?" Phillip forced out tightly.

"As in former lover." He glanced at Lily's ring. "Former fiancé."

"Kenton."

Phillip shot to his feet. "You're the bastard who hurt her. Aren't you?"

Lily stood up and put a hand on his arm. "He's nothing, baby. Certainly not worth bruising your hands for."

Kenton grinned. "Nothing isn't exactly what we used to do with each other."

"Let's go, Phillip."

"I think he should be the one to leave," Phillip said glaring daggers at the man.

Kenton swallowed hard and started backing away. "It's not that serious. I'll go. I'm not going to fight you over her," he said and quickly exited the restaurant.

"Oh, God. I can't believe this," Lily cried.

"Don't cry, sweetheart."

"I don't know what I ever saw in him. I feel ashamed that I even let him touch me."

Lily was silent during the ride to her apartment. And after they got there she remained silent and walked out on the tiny balcony. Phillip came up behind her and wrapped his arms around her waist.

"You belong to me now, tiger Lily. Forget that scumbag. He's not fit to kiss the bottom of your shoe."

"We were engaged for a year when I found out he never had any intentions of marrying me. He just used me until he got tired and then walked away."

"The bastard. I should have–"

"No. You shouldn't. Like he said, he's the former. You're my future. Make love to me, Phillip."

"I promised to shower you with my love. By morning you'll have selective amnesia and all of the bad memories will be permanently erased."

He turned her around to face him and he cupped her face in his two hands and tenderly kissed her lips.

"You are mine, Lily Jordan. Heart body and soul forever. Do you understand me?"

"Oh, yes, my darling man. I more than understand. I'm all yours and only yours forever."

CHAPTER TWENTY-FIVE

Phillip smiled when Lily's head rolled onto his shoulder as she slept while the plane winged them to New Orleans. They'd lingered in Rome for two extra days. He'd met Giovanni and they announced their engagement. Phillip was glad Lily hadn't succumbed to the man's obvious Latin charm. He had to agree that he was a talented designer. When he offered to design a wedding gown for Lily, Phillip hadn't objected, but he was relieved nonetheless when Lily thanked him and said she had someone else in mind to make her wedding gown. She later told Phillip that she wanted Deja Parker to make it. Lily had phoned Deja to insure that she could do it and the gown would be ready in time for the wedding in six weeks.

"What were you thinking just now?" Lily asked sleepily.

"About our wedding and how stunning you're going to look in one of Deja's creations."

"I can hardly wait to be your wife. I love you so much."

He answered her with a kiss. "And I love you."

As Phillip drove through the gates at Magnolia Grove he glanced at Lily. He could tell that she was anxious because she sat fidgeting with the diamond studded locket on the platinum chain he'd bought for her in Rome.

He reached for her hand and squeezed it. "There is nothing to be anxious about."

She shot him an I-don't-quite-believe-you look.

He didn't need to guess what was on her mind.

"My mother is not going to be a problem. Trust me."

When they entered the house and walked into the living room,

Suzette was there enjoying a cup of coffee.

"You're both back. How was your flight?"

Lily wanted to meet her future mother-in-law halfway so she went along with her polite inane conversation.

Phillip let out a sigh of relief, glad they had averted a potentially volatile situation. So far his mother was on her best behavior and he hoped she continued to be so.

"I think you'd better get some rest, Lily. I don't want you to have a relapse."

"Yes, sir, doctor, sir." She saluted him.

"Very funny. Lily."

"All right."

After she had left the room, Phillip turned to his mother. "I'm going up to my room and shower."

"Phillip, I—"

"Lily and I are getting married in six weeks. She'll need help planning the wedding. If you can't bring yourself to do it, I'll get Camille or Jolie."

"I take it you want the wedding to take place at Magnolia Grove?"

"Look, Mother, if—"

"I don't have any objections. I'll offer her my help."

Phillip's eyes narrowed and he gave her a suspicious glance. "I hope you're sincere, Mother."

"I am. I think you're making a mistake, but I know you're not going to listen. So be it."

It wasn't exactly the response he wanted to hear, but it would have to do.

The next morning Lily went to Deja's to choose the perfect wedding dress. She was impressed with the selection.

"You're so talented, Deja. Have you ever thought about displaying your creations at any of the international fashion shows?"

"Who me? Oh, no. That's a little out of my league."

"No. It's not. I've modeled fashions for plenty of the international designers over the years. You're every bit as good if not better than some of them. If you want me to, I can help you get your foot in the door. Your talent will speak for you."

"You really think so? That would be so cool."

Lily smiled. "It would be my pleasure."

"I'm going to design the most beautiful wedding dress you've ever seen, Lily."

"I have every confidence in you, girl."

That afternoon as Lily and Suzette had lunch on the terrace, the older woman approached her about the guest list.

"I put a rush on the invitations. The company I'm using has promised to get them to us in a few days. Of course you'll want to invite your parents personally. I will be sending them a formal invitation as well."

Lily's happy mood disappeared. She wanted to tell her that she'd rather not have them there, but she knew Suzette was watching her and no doubt judging her reaction since she had had her background and relationship with her parents investigated. Lily hoped that if or when they came, they could restrain themselves from arguing long enough to see her get married.

"Is there anyone else you would like to invite? Phillip gave me his list before he left for the hospital."

"Carey Graham and Christine Bradley. I'll personally see that they get theirs."

"I'll be frank with you, Lily. You're not the woman I would have chosen for my son, but I have no say in this. I thought when we talked before you went to Rome you would—never mind. It's water under the bridge. You've agreed to marry him anyway. If you're not willing to have his children I don't hold out much hope for your marriage surviving. That's all I'm going to say on the subject."

"He loves me, Mrs. Cardoneaux."

"And love forgives all things? I hope you're right."

Lily wanted to say something in her defense, but changed her mind. The woman had tunnel vision where she was concerned and couldn't understand and probably never would. They discussed wedding plans, and then Lily went to her room to rest before dinner.

A week later Lily received a phone call.

"Why didn't you call and tell us you were getting married, Lily Ann?" Faye Jordan rebuked her daughter.

"Momma!"

"To receive the invitation in the mail cold like that..."

"I'm sorry if I offended you."

"The invitation didn't offend me, Lily. Your attitude and insensitivity in extending it in that manner did. Why do you always have to get defensive whenever we talk, which isn't very often. You never show me or your father any respect."

"Momma, don't start."

"You haven't called or come to see us in I can't remember when. We've called, left messages and you've never returned even one of them. If I hadn't received that invitation, I was going to call the agency and find out where you were and have it out with you. I want some answers. And I want them now."

"I'm not going to discuss this over the phone."

"I guess it will have to wait until I get there, but make no mistake, we are going to talk, Lily Ann. Your future mother-in-law invited us to stay at Magnolia Grove a week before the wedding. We'll discuss it then."

"Momma. Momma?" Lily heard a loud click and put the receiver on its cradle none too gently. That was all she needed. Maybe she should have gotten married in Rome.

You would eventually have had to see and talk to her and your father.
Why did she have to talk to them? Or see them? It's not as if they

cared what she did. She'd avoided them as much as possible since leaving home ten years ago. And it had been five years since she'd seen either one of her parents. She was sure that nothing had changed. They no doubt still argued all the time about everything.

"Hey, Lily pad. I'm back." Carey laughed as he entered Lily's room through the open French doors.

"Carey, I'm so glad you're here." She rushed over and hugged him.

He frowned, then put her a ways away from him. "Okay, what's wrong?"

"Can't I just be glad to see you? Why does anything have to be wrong?"

"The Dragon Lady isn't still giving you grief. Is she?"

"No. Believe it or not she's been civil."

"Then what is it?"

It's my parents. They're coming to my wedding."

"You thought they wouldn't? You're their only child. Why wouldn't they? What I want to know it why it upsets you so much that they are? I'd say it's about time the three of you talked and tried to work things out."

"You would say that because you just don't understand, Carey."

"Then make me understand, Lily pad. Don't you love your parents?"

"Doesn't everybody?"

"You don't sound like you love yours. Why not?"

"I don't want to get into this with you. It's not going to do any good. It won't change anything."

"It might if you would just-"

"What? Give them a chance? They had their chance when I was growing up."

"That was a long time ago. You're a grown woman now, Lily pad, with a grown woman's insight. Maybe they couldn't talk about it back then. Some parents find it hard to relate to their children on certain levels and subjects. And it's got nothing to do with how they feel about them. I'm sure your parents love you."

"If they do, they have a funny way of showing it."

"I've never seen this side of you, Lily pad. You sound so bitter."

"I guess I am, Carey."

'Maybe when your parents get here you guys can get things out in the open and ease this friction between you."

"I can't see where talking will do any good."

"You'll never know until you try. Think about it. I came out here straight from the airport to see you."

"I appreciate it. Now, how did the shoot go in London?"

"What do you want me to say? It was fantastic? Simone is good, but not as good as you. The shoot went well. Now that you're getting married you and Dr. Phil will be starting a family soon and you'll be ready to retire from modeling anyway."

"We're not going to have any children. I told you that before."

"But you're great with them."

"Yes, when they're somebody else's."

"At the party Dr. Phil gave for you, I heard him say how crazy he was about his niece and nephew, and that he couldn't wait to have children of his own."

"We discussed it."

"And?"

"You're as tenacious as a terrier, Carey. I only agreed to marry him if he understood that there wouldn't be any children."

"He must really love you to agree to those terms."

"He does and I love him all the more for it."

"So where are you two going on your honeymoon?"

"We haven't discussed it. He's already taken time off from the hospital to fly to Rome. He might want to wait and go later." Lily smiled. "What about you and Christine?"

"We're moving right along."

"Is that all you're going to say?"

"At the moment." He grinned. "What you want to know is if it's serious between us, don't you? The answer is it could easily get that way. She's a beautiful person inside and out. Look, I have to go. I'm flying to New York to visit the old homestead."

"Harlem is hardly an old homestead. I'll see you when you get back. You *will* be back in time for the wedding?"

"Wouldn't miss it. I'm taking the wedding pictures."

CHAPTER TWENTY-SIX

Phillip went to Cardoneaux Construction to see his brother.

"Judging from the looks of you, the trip to Rome agreed with you." Nicholas smiled at Phillip as he entered his office.

"Yes, it did. I brought my girl back."

"Sit down. I gathered that when you called me after you returned. About what made her leave in the first place: did you resolve it?"

"Not exactly. She accepted my proposal and we're getting married at Magnolia Grove in six weeks."

Nicholas leaned a hip against his desk and crossed his arms over his chest. "She changed her mind about having children?"

"No. I've decided that I'd rather have just Lily."

"You've always wanted children as much as I have. When you come over and play with Xavier and Solange, I can see the longing in your eyes, Phillip. Are you sure you can do this knowing that you'll be killing any chance of ever being a father?"

"I told you I am."

"You sure you're not just deceiving yourself?"

"I'm positive, Nick. I love Lily, and a life without her is unthinkable. I've already found that out."

"All right. I hope you know what you're doing."

"Believe me, I do. Now, I came here to ask you to be my best man."

"You didn't need to come here and ask me that. You knew what my answer would be."

"I know you have reservations, but I'm glad you're going to do this for me."

"There was never any doubt. You're my brother and I love you. I only want the best for you."

"Believe me, the best thing for me is Lily. You should be getting your official invitation any day. I'm going to call Camille."

"She's been expecting you to. She said you two discussed Lily's negative attitude toward her."

"We did. She wanted to talk to Lily about it, but I didn't think it was a good idea. Now that we are getting married I hope that in time she and Camille will become friends."

"So do I." Nicholas grinned. "Larry and I and Henri are going to throw you a stag party like the one you guys gave me. I'm sure Jamal is going to want to add a few special touches."

"Are you saying that I should beware? We got you to the chapel on time."

"Yes. You did. About Lily, if you're happy, I'm happy for you, little brother." He gave him a bear hug.

"I am, Nick."

It was two weeks before the wedding. Phillip and Lily were having breakfast. His mother had breakfast in her room.

"Are you all right, Lily?" he asked.

"I'm fine." That wasn't exactly true. She was a little nervous, but very excited about the wedding. She was going to marry the man she loved. She blamed her queasy stomach on pre-wedding jitters.

He frowned. You're looking tired. You've probably been over doing." He put on his doctor persona. "I want you to start taking naps in the afternoon. It wasn't that long ago that you were suffering from exhaustion. The last thing I want you to do is have a relapse."

"Phillip, I'm no longer your patient. I'm your fiancée. Okay?"

"All right, I won't nag. I just want you to take care of yourself. Can I pour you a cup of coffee, my dear fiancée?" He lifted the pot to fill her cup.

Lily put her hand over it. "None for me this morning. I'm cutting back on caffeine."

He shot her an questioning glance. "But aren't you the one who doesn't start her day without her morning cup of coffee?"

"Not any more. I've noticed that it's been bothering me lately." She picked up her glass of apple juice. "This is healthier for me. Right, doctor?"

Phillip smiled. "Right." He pushed away from the table. "I've got to be getting to the hospital. When I get home this evening I want you to look over some travel brochures. We haven't had time to discuss where we are going on our honeymoon."

"I didn't think we'd be going on one right away."

"I've already arranged to take two weeks off. Now all we have to do is decide on a place." He bent to kiss her. "See you when I get home. Remember to take that nap."

"Yes, sir."

His smile turned serious. "I mean it, tiger Lily."

"You can take the doctor out of the hospital, but you can't take the hospital out of the doctor."

"I warned you what to expect being the wife of a doctor."

"So you did."

"It's too late to change your mind."

"I have no intention of doing that."

The next day Christine came to see Lily. They had lunch on the terrace.

"I just love the bride's maid dress that Deja created. It follows the theme of your wedding gown to perfection. Her exquisite design is beyond awesome, Lily."

"I agree that she's extremely talented. And I'm going to help her gain the recognition she deserves." The smell of the shrimp salad suddenly made her nauseous and she pushed it away.

"This salad is great. Why aren't you eating yours?"

"I just don't care for it today. Okay?"

"It's not that serious, Lily. You've been kind of edgy lately. Is everything all right between you and the doctor?"

"Oh, yes. I can hardly wait until we're married. I guess I'm suffering from pre-wedding nerves. Carey should be back in a few days, shouldn't he?"

Christine's face lit up. "It can't be soon enough to suit me. I'm really crazy about that man. He said I was beautiful. When I started listing the things I thought weren't, like my mouth is too wide and my eyes are too far apart and a few other things, you know what he said? He loved the way they all came together, making me special."

"I told you he more than likes you. I think the man is in love."

"I hope you're right. Is there anything I can help you with?"

"No. Believe it or not Phillip's mother is handling everything."

"What about your parents?"

"They should be here next week."

"I know you haven't always gotten along. Carey mentioned that—"

"Carey needs to mind his own business."

"He cares about you, Lily. He was only trying to help when he told me about your relationship."

"I can handle my parents."

"Have you and Phillip decided on where you want to go on your honeymoon?"

"We decided to go to Rio for two weeks of fun and sun."

"Mimi told me to tell you that she's sorry that she won't be able to make the wedding, but she's sending you and Phillip a gift."

"I'm glad she let you spend so much time with me."

"She knows I would have taken the time off if she hadn't. I've been officially made Carey's assistant."

"I can see how unhappy you are about that turn of events?"

"Not hardly." She laughed.

"I'm glad you came, Camille. I wouldn't have blamed you if you hadn't considering my attitude toward you," Lily told her.

"Phillip explained that you had hang-ups about children and mixed marriages because of your relationship with your parents."

"That's no excuse for being so rude to you. I'd like to ask a favor of you. I really enjoyed the way you played the piano at the party Phillip gave for me. Would you play at my wedding?"

"I'm glad you liked it. And of course I will. Just tell me what you want me to play."

Lily stood up too quickly and a wave of dizziness assailed her and she swayed.

Camille was at her side in an instant. "Are you all right, Lily?"

"I guess I got up too fast." She sat back down and closed her eyes for a few moments.

"I know you've told Phillip that you don't want any children, but is there a possibility you might be pregnant? I used to have dizzy spells at the beginning of my pregnancy."

"Phillip and I were so careful—except that one time in Rome. Oh, my, God. It can't be. It wasn't the right time of the month."

Camille gave her a sympathetic smile. "Sorry to disabuse you of that particular fantasy, but according to my mother, I was one of the 'it wasn't the right time of the month to get pregnant babies'. How regular are your periods?"

"I'm usually pretty regular, but they have fluctuated the last time or two. According to Phillip, I had been on the verge of a physical breakdown when I collapsed during the photo shoot and landed in the hospital. Surely that wouldn't upset my ovulation cycle."

"I don't know." Camille reached inside her purse and pulled out her cell phone. "I'm going to call my obstetrician, Janet Broussard."

"You don't have to do that."

"Ignorance isn't bliss, Lily. Believe me, I know. You need to know what you're dealing with. It'll alleviate some of the stress." Camille punched in the number and waited. "Janet, this is Camille." She smiled. "I'm fine. This isn't about me. The reason I'm calling is that my future sister-in-law needs to see you right away. Can you squeeze her in today? What about tomorrow morning? At ten?" Camille looked to Lily for confirmation.

Lily nodded.

"Her name is Lily Jordan. Thanks, Janet." Camille ended the call.

"I really appreciate this, Camille. It's probably just nerves and the excitement of getting married that's thrown my system off."

"Tomorrow you'll know for sure. I'll pick you up at nine. Okay?"

"You don't have to take me."

"I know I don't, but I want to."

Dr. Broussard smiled and asked Lily and Camille to have a seat. Camille squeezed Lily's hands and sat in the chair next to hers.

"Your pregnancy test was positive. And judging from my examination, I'd say you were four to five weeks along."

Lily was devastated and didn't immediately respond to the doctor's words.

"How do you feel about the pregnancy? I take it, it wasn't planned?"

"No. I never wanted to have children."

"You have other options."

"You mean abortion?"

"Among others. What about the father? You really should discuss this with him. Camille referred to you as her future sister-in-law. I know Phillip and he'd want to be informed as soon as possible."

"I know he would. The news should make him deliriously happy."

"It's your body and your baby too, Lily. As your doctor, I can only advise you. It's up to you whether you consider any part of that advice. Let me know what you decide."

In the car on the way back to Magnolia Grove, Lily was quiet, contemplative.

Camille pulled over to the side of the street and cut the engine and turned to Lily.

"Would it be so bad having this baby?"

"I know that Phillip will be happy."

"What about how you feel? Don't you think you could love it?"

"I know I could." Tears trickled down her cheeks. "I just didn't ever want to be put in this position. All of the pain I felt growing up seems to have come back to haunt me."

"You and Phillip aren't your parents. Your marriage and your attitude about it is totally different."

"I know what you're trying do, Camille."

"I'm not going to lay any guilt trips on you. This has to be your decision. You and Phillip are the ones who will have to live with it."

CHAPTER TWENTY-SEVEN

Phillip was worried about Lily. She hadn't been acting like herself. She seemed distant and preoccupied. He knew she wasn't thrilled that her parents were coming to the wedding, but he sensed that that wasn't what was bothering her. Whenever he kissed her, she was barely responsive. And when they made love, it was as though her mind was on something else.

One afternoon he came home early and found Lily sitting on a deck chair beneath the boathouse awning just looking out over the River. She was so deep in thought she hadn't heard his approach.

"A penny for your thoughts"

She smiled. "You're home early."

"So are you going to beat me up for it?"

"No, not this time."

"I know your parents will be arriving day after tomorrow. Is that what's bothering you?"

"I am a little apprehensive about it."

"But that's not what's on your mind right now. Is it?"

Lily gazed into his concerned blue eyes. He loved her, she knew that, but she was a little bit resentful because he had made her pregnant and complicated their lives.

You can't lay it all on him. You were a willing participant. You were just as responsible for birth control as he. You know he didn't intentionally forget.

Yes. She knew that. She also knew that she had to tell him about the pregnancy, but she dreaded having the conversation.

"I went to see Janet Broussard last week. According to her calculations, I'm about five weeks pregnant."

Phillip was stunned and dropped into the chair next to Lily's. Her expression was wiped clean of emotion. Of all the things he imagined it could be, that was definitely not one of them. It explained her tiredness lately and her aversion to certain foods. He hoped she didn't think he'd gotten her pregnant on purpose. He knew her views on having children and he would never intentionally disregard her feelings and hurt her or trap her.

"Lily, I don't know what to say. That one time in Rome when you—obviously you were wrong about it not being the right time of the month. I know that's no excuse for my actions."

Lily put her hand over his. "Baby, I know you didn't do it on purpose. Okay? You're too decent a person and too honorable a man to ever do something so underhanded."

Relief washed over his face. "I'm so glad you said that. I wouldn't be honest if I said I wasn't happy about the baby."

"I know."

Phillip's insides roiled at what he knew he had to say.

"Lily, I know you never wanted children. I know there are other alternatives." His breath caught in his throat.

Lily never loved this man more than she did at this very moment. Knowing how much he wanted a baby, she knew how hard it was for him to say those words. He was leaving the decision up to her. She had some serious soul-searching to do.

She leaned over and kissed him tenderly on the lips. "I love you, Phillip Cardoneaux."

"No matter what you decide, I'll always love you, my tiger lily. Having a child is important to me, but not as important as having you in my life. You are my life. I don't want you to forget that."

That night Lily repeatedly turned things over in her mind. She thought about her father. For the first time she could identify with him. He had never wanted children. And after she was born he'd had a vasectomy. He had ignored her, his only child, making her childhood a lonely, indifferent existence. And because her mother had evidently gone against his wishes, their marriage had turned into a battlefield. Only when they were behind closed doors did they call a truce.

Now she herself was facing a similar situation. She hadn't wanted children, but it had been taken out of her hands when she had inadvertently gotten pregnant. But she was in a position to do something to change it. Could she do what it took to remedy the problem? Her whole life hinged on making the right choices.

If you decide to have the baby are you willing to risk your relationship turning into one like your parents have. Could you raise a child the way you were raised? And watch him or her suffer as you did?

What about Phillip, the man you love. This is his child. Can you harm any child belonging to him and expect him to love you afterwards?

He said he'd leave the decision up to me.

But can you hurt him like that? Of course he'll love you, but this one decision will erect an invisible wall between you. Can you handle that, girl?

There was more to consider than just her feelings or Phillip's. Her decision would affect her relationship with the Cardoneaux family.

Suzette was opposed to her marrying Phillip. She'd be happy as a clam if Phillip changed his mind and decided not to go through with the wedding.

Nicholas would probably never forgive her if she decided to abort Phillip's child, killing his brother's chance to be a loving and devoted father. She couldn't blame him for feeling that way.

Camille wouldn't pass judgment, but the fragile new bond of friendship they had so recently forged would suffer.

She had to talk to someone. She needed advice yesterday.

"I was so glad you called, Lily. I'm even happier that you came by," Jolie said ushering her up the stairs to the Puissant's apartment. "I hear distress in you voice. Come on into the kitchen."

Lily followed. She loved the Puissant's kitchen. Today the smell of cinnamon and sugar filled the air.

"I was just baking some cookies for the kids. Sit down while I take the last batch out of the oven."

"I found out I'm pregnant, Jolie."

"Have you told Phillip?"

"Yes. And he's being wonderful about it. As much as he wants the baby, he's leaving the decision up to me as to whether I want to have it or not."

"And are you going to have it?"

Lily didn't answer.

"You evidently haven't decided what you want to do or you wouldn't be looking like you have the weight of the world on your shoulders."

"No. I haven't. There are so many issues I have to resolve before I can begin to decide what I'm going to do."

"One of the most important things you have to do is make peace with you parents. And find out the truth about their marriage not here say from some investigator Suzette Cardoneaux hired." Jolie laughed at Lily's surprised expression.

"Yes, Phillip told me and Henri about it. He was miserable after you left. I know you're bitter about your childhood, but when we're children we see things differently. Our parents are our role models. And sometimes they don't live up to the image we build of them in our minds. We are too immature to realize that they are only human and are bound to make mistakes."

"I wish I had a sister like you, Jolie."

"Feel free to adopt me at any time."

"You're so wise."

Jolie laughed. "Not really. It's just that I've lived longer and experienced more. You'll be able to say that one day. One thing you learned from the investigation is that being black or white really had nothing to do with the relationship between your parents or how they raised you. You had only your aunt's prejudiced perception of the situation."

"I know. Like you said I have to find out the real story from my parents."

"Have I helped at all?"

"More than you realize. You've given me a lot to think about."

"Have a cookie?"

"I was beginning to think you'd never ask."

"Edna said you'd been throwing up this morning," Suzette said to Lily, a ring of concern in her voice. "Are you all right?"

"I'm not dying from a terminal illness if that's what you're worried about. I'm sorry. Forget I said that."

"You're anxious about seeing your parents, aren't you?"

"It's been a while, and as you know we aren't exactly on the best of terms."

"You resent me for prying into your background. And I understand that and I don't blame you. I've been talking to Kyle and he's made me see how unfair I've been to you. He warned me not to go any further with the investigation, but I didn't listen. Phillip is still angry with me for doing it. I don't know if he'll ever forgive me for interfering in his personal life. I thought I was doing it for his own good, but Kyle has made me see I was only doing it for my own selfish reasons. He says I need to curb my control freak tendencies."

Lily smiled. It seemed that Phillip was right about the relationship between his mother and Kyle Barnette. The change in Suzette was miraculous. Lily never expected to hear her apologize for her actions. She hadn't mentioned the baby which meant Phillip hadn't told her. He really was leaving it all up to her, no pressure from any source negative or otherwise.

Lily tensed when she saw her parents enter the airport terminal after disembarking from their plane. They hadn't changed that much since the last time she'd seen them. Her father's hair had more gray mixed in with the blond giving it a silvery appearance. Her mother had gained about ten pounds, but she'd always been a little on the skinny side so the weight was very becoming to her.

Phillip observed Lily's tense features as her parents drew closer, and flashed her a sympathetic smile and gave her hand a supporting squeeze.

David Jordan set his carry on bag down and just looked at his daughter for a few moments, then said.

"I'm so glad to see you, Lily. Over the years when we hadn't heard from or seen you, I worried about you. I know we haven't been close, but you're my only child and I love you." He hugged her. His expression changed when his daughter stiffened. His eyes saddened and he moved back a step.

"You're always hurting either me or your father, Lily Ann," her mother admonished.

"What about all the times you both have hurt me, Momma?"

Phillip recognized the signs of a row building and cleared his throat and stepped between Lily and her parents and extended his hand to David.

"I'm Phillip Cardoneaux, Lily's fiancé, sir."

"Phillip. Call me David."

Phillip smiled at Lily's mother. "I'm pleased to meet you, Mrs. Jordan."

"I'm glad somebody is pleased about that." She shot her daughter a searing look.

"Now, Faye–" David began.

"Don't 'now Faye me', David. Our daughter is being disrespectful as usual. And I don't intend to let her get away with it."

David smiled nervously. "Not here in the airport, Faye."

Lily held her breath waiting for the arguing to start. She was blown away by her mother's next words.

"You're right, David. It can wait until we get to Magnolia Grove."

Phillip saw the relief as well as the confusion on Lily's face. Despite what she'd said about expecting the worst, she'd had expectations that this meeting wouldn't turn into a verbal battle. He also saw the anxious look in her father's eyes. He mentally shook his head. Faye Jordan was evidently very much like her daughter when it came to using bravado to cover her feelings. If there was one needle of hope in this haystack he would find it. There had to be a way to bring Lily and her parents closer together.

CHAPTER TWENTY-EIGHT

Lily studied her parents at dinner that evening. She was still in a state of shock about what didn't happen at the airport earlier. It was hard to believe that her mother hadn't caused a scene. She had actually listened to her husband and taken what he said into consideration before acting. What surprised her most was the fact that she'd done as he had suggested.

Her parents hadn't argued once since they arrived at Magnolia Grove. It was probably just a lull before the storm. But she knew from experience how easily that lull could whip up into hurricane proportions.

While Lily was attempting to analyze them, Phillip was doing a little analyzing of his own: of her. He could almost touch the tension building inside Lily. What happened after dinner would be the acid test. If there were a confrontation, it would most likely be between mother and daughter than with David. There seemed to be more animosity between the two women.

Phillip gazed at the woman he loved. His heart ached for her. She had so much to deal with right now. With all his heart, he wanted Lily to bear their child, but he wanted her to want to so he wouldn't try to pressure her into doing it. He just hoped and prayed that she would decide that she did want to go ahead with the pregnancy.

He focused his attention on Faye and David. A lot was riding on the outcome of the inevitable meeting between the Jordans and their daughter.

Lily glanced at Phillip and smiled. He was a wonderful man. Most men who wanted a child as badly as he did wouldn't have left the decision up to the woman about something like that. He loved and trusted her to make the decision that was right for her despite his own feelings. She realized what a heavy responsibility weighed on her shoulders.

Her happiness was hanging in the balance. She couldn't help picturing a little boy with coal black curly hair that looked exactly like Phillip walking hand and hand with his father. And her heart ached.

Was she being selfish and unfeeling to consider having an abortion, depriving Phillip of being a father? But could she risk possibly raising their child in a house filled with tension if their relationship changed after they had settled into marriage?

She looked at her mother. Had she struggled with herself when she decided to get pregnant without telling her future husband? Why had she risked losing his love? Could it be that she wanted a child with the man she loved so badly that she would go against his wishes? If that were true, it would mean that she really loved her only daughter. But that was impossible, wasn't it? All her life her mother had kept her at an emotional distance. Lily was totally confused now.

She shifted her gaze to her father. He'd said that he had worried about her and he loved her. When he had hugged her, she was caught off guard and had been too stunned to do anything but stiffen in his arms. The look in his eyes said she had deeply wounded him. But he had always resented her, hadn't he? She'd never been a daddy's girl.

Could she possibly have been so wrong about her perception of her parents? Was she losing her mind?

There were too many unanswered questions. Questions she had never thought about asking until now.

It was because you were too cowardly, a little voice taunted.

She and her parents definitely had to talk.

"I noticed that you hardly touched your dinner. Are you feeling all right?" Phillip asked as he entered Lily's room later that evening.

"I wasn't hungry."

"How about now?" he asked as he dropped into the space next to her and wrapped his arms around her waist and lowered her onto the cushion and kissed her.

She smiled. "I'm beginning to have hunger pangs."

"Really. Tell me, my sweet tiger lily, what do you have a taste for?"

"How did you know that I needed you so much, doctor?"

"I have clairvoyant powers as well as medical ones."

"The medical ones I'll believe, but the other... I love you so very much."

"I'm glad you do because I love you as much, probably even more."

"That's not possible."

"Anything is possible the way I feel about you."

Lily eased out of his embrace and got up and walked over to the French doors and looked out on the moonlit garden.

"What is it, Lily?"

"How can you love me considering all I've been putting you through?"

"You're my panacea. Remember? My reality. Anything else is as insubstantial as a dream." He turned her around and kissed her again and again until she quivered with desire, then he slowly undressed her, cherishing every part of her body he uncovered.

Lily undressed him with the same deliberation and love.

When he was completely naked, Phillip lifted her in his arms and carried her over to the bed. He covered her body with his own. With one incredibly deep passionate thrust he made them one. The incredible joy of throbbing flesh moving inside of throbbing flesh, over and over, building the pleasure, driving them past sheer desire, past erotic bliss, beyond rapture. Never had they experienced such complete fulfillment before.

After Phillip had dozed off, Lily watched him sleep and tears spilled down her cheeks. This beautiful man had left his dreams and his heart in her hands. And no matter what she decided, he would accept it because he loved her above all else. It humbled her. She didn't know what she'd done to make him think he loved her that much.

There was something she had to find out before she made her decision.

Lily entered the breakfast room the next morning just as her parents were seating themselves at the table.

An awkward silence pervaded the room.

Lily said good morning and took her place at the table across from

Phillip.

"You look refreshed this morning, " Phillip remarked to the Jordans.

"Oh, we are," David replied. To Suzette, he said. "The suite is splendid, delightfully cool and comfortable. Thank you for inviting us to stay in your home."

"It was my pleasure." Suzette beamed. "If you two would like to, I'd be glad to take you on a tour of Magnolia Grove after you've finished your breakfast.

"Thank you." David smiled. "I'm looking forward to it. My family once owned an estate very much like this one when I was growing up." A nostalgic expression lighted up his features. "Unfortunately it had to be sold. And the new owners turned it into a bed and breakfast."

"Lily mentioned that," Phillip answered. He monitored the looks that passed between mother and daughter. He wanted to stay home from the hospital today. He sensed that Lily might need him.

The remainder of the meal was eaten in silence.

"I have to be going to the hospital. If you need me, Lily, just call me on my cell phone. I'll see you all at dinner." He eased up from his chair and bent to kiss Lily.

She stroked his cheek. "Hurry back."

"I will." Phillip hesitated for a moment before leaving the room.

"Mrs. Cardoneaux, if you wouldn't mind putting off the tour until another time, I'd appreciate it. My parents and I haven't seen each other in a long time and we're eager to catch up on each other's news. You understand."

Suzette shifted her gaze from Lily to her parents and back to Lily.

"No. I don't mind. And yes I do understand. We can do it later this afternoon or tomorrow." She rose from the table. "I need to have a word with Mrs. Bradford about the dinner menu. If you'll excuse me."

No sooner than Suzette had left the room, Faye rounded on her daughter.

"That was rude, Lily Ann. It's no way to treat your fiancé's mother."

"I wasn't being rude, Momma. She knows how anxious I am to talk to you."

"Faye."

"All right, David. Let's get this over with, Lily."

"I think we can be more private down at the gazebo. If you'll just follow me.

Minutes later, Lily opened the gate to the gazebo and signaled for her parents to precede her inside.

Faye took a seat next to David. "All right, Lily Ann. Talk."

"Why don't you love me, Momma?"

"Your mother—"

Lily held up her hand. "Let momma answer, Daddy."

"That's a ridiculous question. You're my daughter," she replied as if that was explanation enough.

"No. It's not, Momma. As far back as I can remember you've let me know that you didn't."

"That's not true."

"Yes. It is. All my friends used to think I had it made because I was an only child and always wore pretty clothes and had every toy I ever wanted. I would have given up all of those things if you had once just told me that you loved me."

Lily shifted her gaze to her father.

"You were just as bad as Momma. You couldn't look at me without thinking how much you wished that I had never been born. The girls at school used to brag about how they could wrap their fathers around their little fingers."

Her lips trembled. "I never said anything because I would have had to confess that my father barely knew I was there and didn't care one way or the other anyway."

"No. Lily, I—"

"I recently found out that you told Aunt Margaret why you could barely stand the sight of me. Momma got pregnant after you had emphatically made it clear that you never wanted children. After I was born you had a vasectomy to insure that it wouldn't happen again. Since you were stuck with me, you made the best of it. I used to think it was because I came out looking more black than white that you didn't love me. That maybe you thought I wasn't really yours."

"My, God, Lily," he choked out. "How could you think that?

192

When did you talk to Margaret?"

"I never actually talked to her personally about it. Phillip's mother didn't trust me and thought I wasn't good enough for him and had my background investigated. Evidently, the private detective she hired spoke to Aunt Margaret and she told him what you told her. And it made sense. Aunt Margaret never could stand me. And now I know why."

"No, it's not the reason you think. Believe me, Lily. Far from it."

"Why should I believe you?"

"Because it's the truth. Before we leave this gazebo you're going to know exactly how I feel and exactly what happened. Now, sit down."

"But, David, I–"

"No, Faye, she needs to know. You're going to have to talk to her too."

Lily sat down and waited.

"I want to start off by saying that your aunt never liked your mother. She thought she wasn't good enough to marry a Jordan. When I met your mother, I thought she was the most beautiful woman in the world. And I wanted her all to myself. I realized later how selfish I'd been. I thought children would come between us. I made it a condition of our getting married and that was wrong. I knew that she wanted children since she herself had been an only child.

"I'd been raised with four sisters and three brothers in Georgia. Both of my parents had to work long hours to take care of all of us which meant there was hardly ever any time for us to bond as a family. What little time they had together was usually spent arguing about whose fault it was to have children in the first place. I began to see that having children was a burden and decided I never wanted to have any of my own. When I married I wanted my wife's full attention.

"I met your mother when I went away to college and later on to law school. While I was studying at the library, I talked to her and really got to know her."

David looked at Faye fondly and squeezed her hand.

For the first time Lily noticed the love he obviously felt for his wife shining in his eyes.

"I was fascinated by her dusky cinnamon brown skin and dark

nearly black eyes. I knew the moment I met her that she was the one woman for me and I wanted her all to myself. When Margaret found out the woman I loved was black, she had a fit and accused me of being disloyal to our heritage. Of all my sisters I was closest to her. She was the eldest and was the next best thing to being a mother I ever had. I loved and respected her. I told her I wanted to marry your mother. She said she'd never forgive me if I did.

"Your mother and I had been lovers for a few months when I brought up the subject of getting married. When I told her that I didn't want children, she started crying and blurted out that she thought she might be pregnant. I was stunned. We'd been so careful about birth control and here she was telling me it had failed. I got angry and accused her of deliberately getting pregnant. She swore that it was an accident. I didn't believe her. God forgive me, I told her to get an abortion. No. I didn't *tell* her I *demanded* that she get one. She refused. Nothing I said would sway her. I got drunk one night and went to my sister's house. I ended up telling her everything."

"Then what happened?"

David stood up and started pacing.

"Since I loved your mother and she was carrying my child, I decided that we should get married. As the pregnancy progressed I grew resentful. After you were born my resentment grew. Babies needed a lot of attention and it seemed to me that your mother was giving every scrap of her attention and affection to the new baby and there was none left for me. I started working late, and your mother complained that I was never home anymore. I told her it was her fault. And we argued. After that it seemed it was all we ever did.

"Do you remember when you were seven and your mother got sick and we sent you to stay with Margaret for a while?"

"Yes. I remember. I was miserable. I could tell that she didn't like me. When my cousins came over she treated them differently than she treated me. I overheard her telling Aunt Rose that you never should have married a scheming black woman because your children wouldn't be white, and you'd never know if they were yours."

"Oh, God. I never knew that. Why didn't you tell me, Lily?"

"I thought it was the reason why you ignored me."

"No. It wasn't. I was a selfish bastard. By the time I realized what I was doing to you. It was too late. I tried so many times after that to reach you, but you tuned me out."

"Aunt Margaret told the investigator that you had a vasectomy. Was it because you wanted to make sure there were no more children?"

"I could strangle Margaret for saying that. I had it done because your mother couldn't take the pill and condoms, as you know, aren't a hundred per cent reliable. Back then they were even less so. The reason your mother was sick was because she'd had an IUD inserted and it caused an infection. The doctors didn't want to perform a tubal ligation because she'd only had one child. I didn't want to risk her life so I had the vasectomy. I don't care what Margaret said, it wasn't because I didn't trust your mother not to purposely get pregnant. You were precious to us Lily, especially to your mother. I realized when I had the vasectomy there really wouldn't be any more children. And that I would get what I had once wished for now that I didn't want it. Those first seven years were hell. Mostly my fault. You were caught in the middle and we ignored your pain, selfishly concentrating on our own, putting our own wants and desires before yours. And for that I'm truly sorry. You did what any child would do. You tuned us out. Can you ever forgive us?"

"Lily Ann, I should have been there for you, but I was wrapped up in my own misery. When David accused me of getting pregnant on purpose, it hurt. I wanted children true enough, but I would never have done that. Of course Margaret didn't help. At every turn she maligned me to your father and any member of the Jordan family who would listen.

Faye walked over to Lily and sat down next to her. "I always loved you, baby. For a while I let the resentment I felt toward your father for believing that about me to ruin our life together. The only time and place we didn't argue was in the bedroom. We were selfish, Lily. What can I say? I realized how much we'd hurt you when you couldn't wait to get away from us. We tried to get you to come home.

Whenever we suggested coming to see you, you told us not to.

It was like you were trying to X us out of your life. We knew then how deeply we'd hurt you and we couldn't do anything to reverse the damage."

David took Lily's hand in his. "We wanted to make it up to you, Lily, but it was too late. You didn't trust us. You're all grown up now and about to be married. When we got that invitation, cold like that, we knew what you thought of us."

"As usual I overreacted when I saw you," Faye confessed.

"Phillip says I do the same thing," Lily admitted.

"I know it's going to take time, but do you think–"

"I don't know, Daddy. For so long I've thought that you hated me. Momma, I thought you resented me for coming between you and daddy. And to find out–"

"We were so into ourselves and our problems we were oblivious to your pain. By the time we realized it, we'd ruined your childhood. We should have let you know that we loved you. It's a time we can never get back."

"Trust is the most important part of love, Lily. If I'd trusted and believed in your mother things would have turned out differently.

David pulled the two most important people in his life into his arms.

CHAPTER TWENTY-NINE

"You were so quiet at dinner." Phillip entered the gazebo and walked over to where Lily sat and dropped into the seat next to her. "I gather that you had that talk with your parents. Are you all right?"

"Yes."

"How did it go?"

"Better than I dared to hope. Jolie was right when she said we see our parents through a child's eye. Even when we get older it's hard to see them as human beings who had a life before you entered it and that they do make mistakes."

"Is that what happened to you? You perceive them in a different light now?"

"Yes. All my life I thought it was a black and white thing, or a mixed marriage disaster, when it really wasn't. It's part of the reason why I didn't want to have children. Maybe to my Aunt Margaret it was a disgrace to marry someone of another race, but my father never felt that way. All this time I thought my mother had purposely gotten pregnant, and because my father didn't want more children, I thought it was because they both wished I had never been born. But I was wrong, Phillip." She went on to relate what her parents had told her.

"I realize that our having children or not having children should be a personal decision between the two of us. What we need to do is truly and deeply trust each other. How and in what emotional atmosphere we raise our children is up to us. It would be up to us to show them how much we love them."

Phillip's heart was near to bursting at her words.

"Deep down I never really wanted an abortion. I wanted our baby, but I was afraid we might scar it if our relationship changed into something distant and cold."

"I knew how afraid you were. It wasn't a fear I could make go away.

It savaged me that I couldn't heal your wounds. I knew the only way you could begin to heal was to talk to your parents and really understand what made them react to you the way they had."

"I'm sorry for putting you through this."

"It was something you had to personally resolve. You weren't doing it to hurt me."

"You're such a wonderful man, Phillip Cardoneaux. I don't deserve you."

"We are made for one another, tiger lily. And in four days I'm going to make you my wife."

"I love hearing those words."

"Tiger lily?"

She punched him in arm. "No. The part about becoming your wife." Lily stood up and Phillip followed suit. She started unbuttoning his shirt.

"You think to get a jump on the wedding night. Is that it?"

"You did say that practice makes perfect. Didn't you?"

"I vaguely remember saying that."

Lily took his hand and tugged him toward the gate of the gazebo.

"Where are we going?"

"Down to the pool to cool off."

"You mean cool down. I definitely have the hots for you, lady."

"And I hope you always will."

He had waited for this day all his adult life. In a few moments, the woman of his dreams would enter the room and march down the aisle to be his wife. His mother had outdone herself with the preparations for the wedding. She'd turned the ballroom into a wedding chapel. The chairs were arranged on either side of the aisle she'd created. He smiled as the music began to play the special song Camille had written for the wedding.

His mother was holding Solange and Kyle, Xavier. He shook his head. She and Kyle were contemplating marriage. He couldn't be happier for them. He laughed remembering a conversation he'd had with Kyle.

"You think you can handle her?" Phillip had asked.

"I don't really want to handle her. I just want to help her realize that she doesn't have to be in control of the lives of everyone she loves. And that she deserves a life of her own and I want her to share it with me."

"You're a good man. And a brave one," he'd quipped. You're exactly what she needs."

"I agree."

"Are you sure you know what you're getting into? She can be a real vixen."

"What you mean is she's going to be a real challenge. I think I'm up for it."

Camille started playing. And Phillip waited for his bride to appear. His breath caught in his throat when Lily and her father started down the aisle. The dress Deja created for her was a work of art. But the woman David and Faye had created was the real masterpiece. The delicate champagne color of the toga-inspired design complimented Lily's beautiful brown skin and shiny blonde-streaked brown hair which was done in a Greek cluster atop her head with long loose spiral curls hanging down her back.

The brilliant, loving smile turning up the corners of her lips when her gaze met his threw everything and everybody in the background.

This was the woman he loved and who loved him. She was carrying the child of their love beneath her heart. His world was complete.

Lily had never dreamed that she could ever be this happy a few weeks ago. She glanced at her mother and saw the tears in her eyes. She saw something else. She saw the love and pride she'd waited all her life to see shining there. She now understood so much about her parents and their feelings for each other and for her.

To Lily herself it was hard to fathom that she had ever considered for even one moment not having the baby. The thought still made her shudder.

She shifted her attention to the man she loved. He was devastatingly handsome and looked so incredibly sexy in his tuxedo it took her breath away.

Phillip and Lily barely heard the words the minister was saying. In their hearts they were already man and wife. This ceremony just made it official.

"Do you Phillip Jacques Cardoneaux take Lily Ann Jordan to be your wife?"

Phillip smiled. "I do."

"Do you Lily Ann Jordan take Phillip Jacques Cardoneaux to be your husband."

Lily's voice trembled. "I do with all my heart."

"The rings. Nicholas placed them on the bible the minister held.

Phillip lifted Lily's finger and slid her ring onto it. Lily slid the ring she'd gotten for Phillip on his finger.

"As you have promised to love, honor and cherish each other for the rest of your lives, I now pronounce you husband and wife. Phillip, you may now kiss your bride."

Phillip reverently cupped Lily's face in his two hands and gently kissed her lips.

Carey caught the moment on film, as well as the joys moments that followed as everyone gathered around the happy couple.

Seven months and two weeks later Lily gave birth to Andre Phillip Cardoneaux, who was the image of his father, only with honey-gold skin.

ABOUT THE AUTHOR

Working in the editorial department of the L.A. *Herald Examiner* gave **Beverly Clark** her first exposure to professional writing. And from there she wrote fillers for the newspaper and magazines such as *RedBook, Good Housekeeping and McCalls*. She plied her writing talent, penning and getting published one hundred twenty romantic short-stories with Sterling/MacFadden Magazines.

Beverly joined RWA, a national writer's organization that helps writers, both published and unpublished, reach their writing goals. To gain more knowledge of the writing craft she attended creative writing classes at Antelope Valley College. And to keep up with the ever changing writer's market, she attends writing conferences, classes and seminars at L.T.U. She has since completed eight full length books. Beverly once managed a second-hand book store, The Book Nook, for two years. In doing so, she became adept at reading the book buying market. She also helped a group called Friends of the Libraries, encouraging children and adults to read and enjoy books.. She now lives in Los Angeles.

Beverly has completed four book contracts with Genesis Press. Her first included two contemporary romances, *Yesterday Is Gone* released June '97 and *A Love to Cherish* August of '98. *A Love to Cherish* was featured in Black Expression Book Club. Her second contract for *The Price of Love* was completed and the book released March '99. Her third contract was for *Bound by Love* released June 2000. *Cherish the Flame*, Feb of 2002. Jan of 2003 *A Twist of Fate* and Feb 2005 *Echoes of Yesterday*.

Excerpt from

TIMELESS DEVOTION

BY

BELLA MCFARLAND

Release Date: August 2005

CHAPTER 1

Don't worry if you don't hear from me for awhile, Cat. I'm going to New York. I'll talk to you when I get back. Bobby.

Once again, Cat Simmons reread the brief note her brother had left in her mailbox. A deep sigh escaped her. She didn't know what else to do to help him deal with their mother's death or the events that took place prior to it.

"Rereading it over and over again will not make it go away, Cat," her best friend Jan said from behind her.

Pushing the note into the pocket of her jumpsuit, Cat pivoted around to face Jan. A frown settled on her walnut-brown face. "I know. I've been thinking, though. I want to hire an investigator to help Bobby. He's so obsessed with finding this…this *fictitious* biological father that nothing I say seems to penetrate."

"I thought you said you didn't want to validate his crazy notion that your mother had…" Jan bit her bottom lip, a little uncertain about broaching the sensitive subject.

"Just say it, Jan. That my mother had cheated on my father, and that Bobby was the result of that affair. No, I don't want to. But Bobby believes it's true. He's hurting, Jan, refuses to discuss things with Dad or Kenny. I'm all he has." Cat massaged her temple and took a deep, calming breath. She couldn't afford to be distracted or worked up over this, not when she was about to perform a stunt. Most stunts needed total concentration and precision. Thinking about her personal problems before or during a performance could only lead to disaster. Still, she couldn't help worrying about her little brother. "If I can't convince him to stop this madness, the least I can do is help him. As soon as I'm done here, I'm going to search the yellow pages for a private investigator." She picked up her Neumann's skydiving gloves from the dresser, slipped them on, and adjusted the straps. "What do you think?"

"Sounds like a great idea," Jan said. "Count me in." Cat frowned at her. "Quit scowling at me. That boy is like a brother to me, okay? Besides, private investigators don't come cheap. So count me in."

Emotions blocked Cat's throat. Friends like Jan were hard to find. Jan was one of the few African-American actresses with a lead role in a hit T.V. series. They'd met at a performing art camp at UCLA years ago and had become fast friends. Nevertheless, Cat couldn't allow Jan to pay for something that didn't concern her family. "Thanks, Jan, but I should be able to take care of it."

"Sure?"

Cat nodded.

"Okay. But know that I've got your back covered if things get a little tight." Jan opened a bag of cheese doodles and pushed one into her mouth.

"I know." Cat's eyes followed Jan's hand as it dipped into the bag and pulled out another doodle. "How can you eat that stuff?"

Jan shrugged her thin shoulders. "Easily. Just pop one in my mouth, munch, and swallow. Speaking of eating, are you coming to my dinner party tomorrow night? I have a yummy date for you."

Cat rolled her eyes. "I told you, woman, I'm through dating. No more handsome men with wicked smiles or cute butts. No more dealing with cocky attitudes or excusing bad habits."

Jan pointed an orange-stained finger at Cat. "Cute butts, Cat? Come on, you are a sucker for a guy with a firm behind, and you know it."

"I was. I'm cured." Her ex-boyfriend, Rick, had made sure of that. "Did I tell you Rick used my credit card without my knowledge? And do you know why I didn't see that coming? His cute butt got in the way, that's why." And because she'd allowed her feelings to get involved, she added silently.

"It's been six months, Cat, let it go. Cancel your credit cards and let your lawyer deal with Rick."

"Already did."

"Well, then, that's that. Now about tomorrow's dinner… If you don't make it, sweetie, I'll have an unpaired male on my hands, a hostess's nightmare." Jan popped another doodle into her mouth, then rolled the bag and dropped it on the table. She turned her famous hazel eyes on Cat. "Please, Cat. Please. I really, really need you."

Cat checked the zippers on her red jumpsuit and then reached for her goggles. "Okay. But you'll owe me big time for this, Janelle Masters."

"Oh, thank you." Jan blew her a kiss and jumped to her feet.

"Bailing you out should be added to my things-*not*-to-do list."

Jan merely grinned at her words.

"So tell me more about this blind date you're saddling me with. What does he do?"

"Works in a bank," Jan answered as she padded to the fridge to get bottled water. She closed the door with her hip and then she leaned against it.

"Good. That means he's conservative, no braided or dreadlocked hair."

Jan rolled her eyes.

"I'm through with men who thumb their noses at society," Cat added.

"Another one of your rules?"

"You've got it. What else can you tell me about him?"

"He went to school with my man, so he's decent."

Cat snickered. "FYI, Miss Movie Star, Doug is as bad-ass as they come. Don't use him as a yardstick." She pushed the goggles up in her hair. She was reaching for her helmet when a masterful purr of a V-twin engine sounded outside the trailer. When Jan looked out the window, Cat asked, "Is that him out there?"

"Doug? Are you kidding? My man knows I can't abide motorbikes. But you'd better take a long, hard look, girl, because if you're serious about all those rules you keep spouting, you're about to miss out."

"Why? Who is it?" Cat asked as she approached the window.

"The kind of bad boy you've sworn to steer clear of."

Cat moved forward to take a look at what had her friend grinning like a well-fed cat.

My, oh my, what a beauty, Cat sighed as her eyes followed the Harley-Davidson with its two-tone sterling silver and vivid black lines. What she wouldn't give to ride that, she mused longingly.

Then her eyes moved to the owner of the bike as he switched off the engine and stood up. Watching him dismount sent a thrill through her that had nothing to do with the bike. Now riding that, Cat mused, would be more exciting and dangerous than her most daring stunt.

He was big. All she could see was his masculine back, powerful thighs molded by black jeans, scruffy boots and a leather jacket that had seen better days. Jet black, curly hair fell over his broad shoulders. Wonder how it would feel to run fingers through it? Cat mused.

As if to tease her already heightened senses, the man turned and gave her a side profile. Rich chocolate skin, proud bearing, strong nose, and a two-day shadow, she noted. If only she could see the rest of his face. Still, the sigh that escaped her lips was close to a purr.

"Quit licking your lips, Catherine. Go out there and prove me wrong."

Cat's head snapped toward her friend as a feeling close to panic washed over her. That man was too much for her to test her theory on. She stalled. "Prove what?"

"That you're immune to *that* gorgeous hunk. Damn, he makes me want to crawl into his pants."

Me too, Cat added silently. Who was he? An actor?

A knock on the trailer door interrupted her musing. One of the makeup artists, Iryna Chekhov, stepped inside the trailer when Jan bid her to come in. "Sorry to interrupt, Jan. Jed Sutton needs Cat now. The plane will be taking off in ten minutes."

"Thanks, Iryna. I'm right behind you."

As if that were her cue, Iryna stepped down from the trailer and disappeared.

"I've got to go, Jan. No time for testing theories."

"Chicken." Jan picked her car keys up from the table and threw them to her. "Take care of my baby, sweetie. Drop it off at my place tomorrow night when you come to dinner."

Cat caught the keys and nodded. They'd used Jan's car to get to the filming location, but since Doug was picking Jan up, she had offered to drive her car back to Los Angeles. As she moved toward the door, the biker outside intruded on her thoughts.

No man was going to turn her into a coward, Cat decided, no matter how gorgeous he looked. "Okay, Jan. Watch and weep. I'm going out there to have a normal conversation with that handsome...*renegade*."

Jan guffawed.

"Then I'm going to leave without a backward glance," Cat added.

"I'll be watching. Make sure you come back in one piece, you hear."

Cat rolled her eyes. "Please. He's just a man."

"I meant the skydiving, silly. See, he's already making you forget what we're doing here. Look at me, sweetie. We are at Edwards Air Force Base jump field to film a movie." Jan spaced her words as if she were talking to a confused person, and she added sign language for effect. "You are about to hurtle to earth at a death-defying speed, doubling for *moi*, your best friend."

"Very funny." Cat picked up her helmet and opened the trailer door.

"Jokes aside, Cat, be careful."

Jan always wished her good luck whenever she was about to do a stunt, Cat thought with a smile. They were tight like that. "Will do," Cat answered. Then she left the trailer.

—m—

Taj Taylor stared with amazement at the people scurrying about the jump field. Were all location film sites this chaotic? How the hell was he going to locate the producer, Dorian McCarthy?

"Nice ride," a voice said from behind him.

His head snapped toward the soft, feminine voice. A stunning woman in a red skydiving suit was standing near the entrance of a trailer, her eyes trained on his bike. As he took in her exotic brown face— the long, graceful neck, the delicately molded short nose, the sensually lush lips, and the high cheekbones—his stomach lurched, as if he were about to take a plunge off an endless precipice. Ignoring the feeling, he murmured, "Thank you."

Cat stepped closer to the bike. "A 1340 Evolution engine?"

Very intriguing, Taj mused. He hadn't met that many women who were interested in motorbikes, let alone able to identify a particular engine. "A modified 1340."

"Impressive. Recorded maximum performance yet?"

She had him totally enthralled now. Who was she? "A maximum of 165 horsepower. You obviously know your motorbikes."

"I've ridden some, modified a few. Yours is a real beauty."

Why didn't she look at him? His bike was getting all her attention, darn it. "Power and beauty are an irresistible combination. I'm a sucker for both."

She flashed a smile his way. "Obviously. How does it handle long distance?"

Still reeling from the effect of her smile, Taj said the first thing that popped into his head. "Purrs like a satiated lover." Her head snapped toward him, and their eyes met. Hers were dark and mysterious. They seemed to sear right through him to his very soul. When her eyebrows shot up, he realized what he'd said. "Handle her with care, and she'll give you the best ride of your life." Damn, that didn't come out well either.

Taj was sure the woman would comment on his sexist remarks, but all she did was shift her slender body until she was facing him. Then she proceeded to study him. A laconic smile passed her lips as she took in his two-day stubble. Made him wish he'd shaved before driving out to see McCarthy. His shoulder-length curly hair received a frown before her eyes ran down his frame. For once, he was happy he hit the gym regularly.

When she said, "Nice chatting with you," and sashayed past him, Taj didn't say anything. Couldn't say anything was more like it. He was still trying to find his balance.

His gaze followed her delectable form. He hoped, no, prayed she would look back. *Come on, baby, just once,* he urged silently. She never looked back.

Taj shook his head to clear it. He didn't know what had just happened, but he was now more interested in what McCarthy wanted from him than before. He hadn't been too keen on taking the assignment, but if it meant knowing the identity of that exquisite creature, he would make time.

"Excuse me?" A man wearing a security badge interrupted his musing. "This area is off-limits, sir."

Taj handed him his card. "I'm here to see Dorian McCarthy."

The guard studied the card. "You need to talk to Mr. Gunter, the unit manager. No one sees McCarthy without going through him."

He'd made the necessary adjustments in his schedule for this detour, Taj reflected, and the last thing he needed was to be given the runaround. On the other hand, he couldn't take out his frustrations on a guy following orders. "Okay, my friend, take me to Mr. Gunter."

"They're actually all together over there." The guard pointed at a group of four men and a woman standing at the edge of the field.

"Which one is McCarthy?"

"Red hair and goatee, hard to miss," the guard answered.

Squinting against the glaring sun, Taj focused his gaze on the group. As the guard had said, it was hard not to notice Dorian McCarthy. He was dressed in white pants and white shirt, and had an unruly mop of red hair. A narrow moustache sat above his lips. He was in his mid-fifties, Taj recalled from the background information he'd gotten over the Internet, although looking at him you'd never guess it. He was of slight built and in pretty good shape.

McCarthy had become a household name in the eighties when he'd produced one action-packed blockbuster after another. Then he'd made the fatal error of switching to romantic comedies. Bad reviews and box office disasters had followed. As if that were merely a prelude to worse times, he'd gotten involved in a scandalous affair with an aspiring actress and ended up in court, fighting for his reputation and his children. His ex-wife, a daughter of a well-known Hollywood mogul, had made sure that he paid. By the time the messy divorce was over, Dorian had become a pariah in Hollywood.

"Wait here, Mr. Taylor." The guard went directly to a gangly man in a Dodgers baseball cap, and handed him Taj's card. After a brief consultation, the man spoke to McCarthy, who looked up.

"Ah, Mr. Taylor, I've been expecting you." McCarthy excused himself from his colleagues, and drew Taj aside. "I'm happy you made it." He paused to study Taj with pursed lips and a thoughtful expression. "Ever thought of being in the movies, Mr. Taylor?"

Taj's eyebrows shot up. "Not really."

"I was told that you're a former FBI agent. Ever consulted for a movie company?"

Taj studied the older man and wondered where the interrogation was headed. "No. Look, Mr. McCarthy, from the message you left with my secretary, I had the impression that you desperately needed my expertise."

McCarthy nodded his head. "But I do, Mr. Taylor. I need a consultant, someone who can give me the inside info on how the Bureau profiles criminals, how a killer's mind works."

Taj's heart sank at McCarthy's words. This was the very reason he had left the Bureau. He'd gotten tired of delving into the twisted minds of criminals. Taj shook his head. "Mr. McCarthy, I've got to be honest with you. I stopped profiling criminals a long time ago."

"But I bet you haven't forgotten the training. I know what you're thinking," the producer said, his eyes sparkling with enthusiasm. "It's just a movie, right? Actors pretending to be agents, nothing like the real thing. Well, Mr. Taylor, we want it to be as close to the real thing as possible. With your help, we can do it. I want the audiences spooked when they watch the antics of the psycho in the *The Gardian* and rooting for my lead actress and her supporting actor, and I can't do it without you, Mr. Taylor."

Taj's brows furrowed. The last thing he wanted to revisit was his FBI days. But at the same time, there was the exquisite woman he'd met earlier. "What happened to the consultant you had before. I assume you hired one before you started filming."

McCarthy rolled on his heels and gave Taj a wry smile. "Oh, yes, we had one. A friend recommended him, and I went along because he had the credentials. He turned out to be unreliable, irresponsible, and a difficult man to work with. I need your help, Mr. Taylor. Jackie Wilson told me you were the best there is."

Taj smiled. Jackie Wilson was a former client of his, an aging African-American diva who'd conquered Broadway before coming to Hollywood. "I see," was all he said.

"She said I could count on you to see us through this fiasco. Of course," McCarthy hastened to add, "we'll work around your schedule and compensate you for any jobs you could be working on in the next two weeks."

"That won't be necessary, Mr. McCarthy. My people can handle things without me."

McCarthy perked up. "Do I take it that you're coming aboard?"

Taj smiled at his reaction. "Yes."

"Oh, that's wonderful!" He reached for Taj's hand and pumped it vigorously. We're going to have a ball making…oh, excuse me. I need to answer this." He raised the receiver end of the walkie-talkie to his ear. "Yes? Go ahead. Give him whatever he wants…two extra parachutes if it makes him happy."

Dorian turned to whisper to Taj, "I got Pierce Quinn as my lead actor. Lots of talent there. I tell you, he's the next Colin Farrell. Yes?" he murmured into the mouthpiece. "Have Cat talk to him. She already did? Okay, I'll be there." Dorian turned to Taj, "I've got to go. We need to go with the first take on this. Thanks for joining us, Mr. Taylor."

Taj nodded curtly. "I have a quick question, Mr. McCarthy."

"Shoot."

"Is the lead actress doing the stunts with Pierce Quinn?"

"Janelle Masters doesn't do her own stunts, my friend. The woman in red is just a double, a stuntwoman by the name of Cat Simmons. You'll meet them all at the studio on Monday." They shook hands. "Listen, I appreciate your going out of your way today, Mr. Taylor. I'll stop by your offices later and finalize everything."

Taj watched the producer dash across the field to join the people around the plane. He could see the figure in red. She was in a deep discussion with another man. Cat Simmons, stuntwoman.

Just a double wasn't the expression he'd use to describe Cat. In fact, he had known there was something special about her the moment he'd laid eyes on her, Taj reflected as he headed back to his bike. Cat was no one's double. She was special. Even her name, Cat, was unique.

Instead of starting his bike and leaving, Taj settled on it and watched the scene unfold on the field before him. Someone made an announcement, and everyone cleared the field. The plane took off and steadily gained altitude. He could feel the tension and the excitement in the observers. He too felt a tinge of anticipation at the thought of seeing Cat Simmons in action.

BEYOND THE RAPTURE

2005 Publication Schedule

January

A Heart's Awakening
Veronica Parker
$9.95
1-58571-143-8

Falling
Natalie Dunbar
$9.95
1-58571-121-7

February

Echoes of Yesterday
Beverly Clark
$9.95
1-58571-131-4

A Love of Her Own
Cheris F. Hodges
$9.95
1-58571-136-5

Higher Ground
Leah Latimer
$19.95
1-58571-157-8

March

Misconceptions
Pamela Leigh Starr
$9.95
1-58571-117-9

I'll Paint a Sun
A.J. Garrotto
$9.95
1-58571-165-9

Peace Be Still
Colette Haywood
$12.95
1-58571-129-2

April

Intentional Mistakes
Michele Sudler
$9.95
1-58571-152-7

Conquering Dr. Wexler's Heart
Kimberley White
$9.95
1-58571-126-8

Song in the Park
Martin Brant
$15.95
1-58571-125-X

May

The Color Line
Lizzette Grayson Carter
$9.95
1-58571-163-2

Unconditional
A.C. Arthur
$9.95
1-58571-142-X

Last Train to Memphis
Elsa Cook
$12.95
1-58571-146-2

June

Angel's Paradise
Janice Angelique
$9.95
1-58571-107-1

Suddenly You
Crystal Hubbard
$9.95
1-58571-158-6

Matters of Life and
   Death
Lesego Malepe, Ph.D.
$15.95
1-58571-124-1

2005 Publication Schedule (continued)

July

Class Reunion
Irma Jenkins/John
　Brown
$12.95
1-58571-123-3

Wild Ravens
Altonya Washington
$9.95
1-58571-164-0

August

Path of Thorns
Annetta P. Lee
$9.95
1-58571-145-4

Timeless Devotion
Bella McFarland
$9.95
1-58571-148-9

Life Is Never As It Seems
J.J. Michael
$12.95
1-58571-153-5

September

Beyond the Rapture
Beverly Clark
$9.95
1-58571-130-6

Blood Lust
J. M. Jeffries
$9.95
1-58571-138-1

Rough on Rats and
　Tough on Cats
Chris Parker
$12.95
1-58571-154-3

October

A Will to Love
Angie Daniels
$9.95
1-58571-141-1

Taken by You
Dorothy Elizabeth Love
$9.95
1-58571-162-4

Soul Eyes
Wayne L. Wilson
$12.95
1-58571-147-0

November

A Drummer's Beat to
　Mend
Kei Swanson
$9.95
1-58571-171-3

Sweet Reprecussions
Kimberley White
$9.95
1-58571-159-4

Red Polka Dot in a
　World of Plaid
Varian Johnson
$12.95
1-58571-140-3

December

Hand in Glove
Andrea Jackson
$9.95
1-58571-166-7

Blaze
Barbara Keaton
$9.95
1-58571-172-1

Across
Carol Payne
$12.95
1-58571-149-7

Other Genesis Press, Inc. Titles

Acquisitions	Kimberley White	$8.95
A Dangerous Deception	J.M. Jeffries	$8.95
A Dangerous Love	J.M. Jeffries	$8.95
A Dangerous Obsession	J.M. Jeffries	$8.95
After the Vows	Leslie Esdaile	$10.95
(Summer Anthology)	T.T. Henderson	
	Jacqueline Thomas	
Again My Love	Kayla Perrin	$10.95
Against the Wind	Gwynne Forster	$8.95
A Lark on the Wing	Phyliss Hamilton	$8.95
A Lighter Shade of Brown	Vicki Andrews	$8.95
All I Ask	Barbara Keaton	$8.95
A Love to Cherish	Beverly Clark	$8.95
Ambrosia	T.T. Henderson	$8.95
And Then Came You	Dorothy Elizabeth Love	$8.95
Angel's Paradise	Janice Angelique	$8.95
A Risk of Rain	Dar Tomlinson	$8.95
At Last	Lisa G. Riley	$8.95
Best of Friends	Natalie Dunbar	$8.95
Bound by Love	Beverly Clark	$8.95
Breeze	Robin Hampton Allen	$10.95
Brown Sugar Diaries &	Delores Bundy &	$10.95
Other Sexy Tales	Cole Riley	
By Design	Barbara Keaton	$8.95
Cajun Heat	Charlene Berry	$8.95
Careless Whispers	Rochelle Alers	$8.95
Caught in a Trap	Andre Michelle	$8.95
Chances	Pamela Leigh Starr	$8.95
Dark Embrace	Crystal Wilson Harris	$8.95
Dark Storm Rising	Chinelu Moore	$10.95
Designer Passion	Dar Tomlinson	$8.95
Ebony Butterfly II	Delilah Dawson	$14.95

Erotic Anthology	Assorted	$8.95
Eve's Prescription	Edwina Martin Arnold	$8.95
Everlastin' Love	Gay G. Gunn	$8.95
Fate	Pamela Leigh Starr	$8.95
Forbidden Quest	Dar Tomlinson	$10.95
Fragment in the Sand	Annetta P. Lee	$8.95
From the Ashes	Kathleen Suzanne	$8.95
	Jeanne Sumerix	
Gentle Yearning	Rochelle Alers	$10.95
Glory of Love	Sinclair LeBeau	$10.95
Hart & Soul	Angie Daniels	$8.95
Heartbeat	Stephanie Bedwell-Grime	$8.95
I'll Be Your Shelter	Giselle Carmichael	$8.95
Illusions	Pamela Leigh Starr	$8.95
Indiscretions	Donna Hill	$8.95
Interlude	Donna Hill	$8.95
Intimate Intentions	Angie Daniels	$8.95
Just an Affair	Eugenia O'Neal	$8.95
Kiss or Keep	Debra Phillips	$8.95
Love Always	Mildred E. Riley	$10.95
Love Unveiled	Gloria Greene	$10.95
Love's Deception	Charlene Berry	$10.95
Mae's Promise	Melody Walcott	$8.95
Meant to Be	Jeanne Sumerix	$8.95
Midnight Clear	Leslie Esdaile	$10.95
(Anthology)	Gwynne Forster	
	Carmen Green	
	Monica Jackson	
Midnight Magic	Gwynne Forster	$8.95
Midnight Peril	Vicki Andrews	$10.95
My Buffalo Soldier	Barbara B. K. Reeves	$8.95
Naked Soul	Gwynne Forster	$8.95
No Regrets	Mildred E. Riley	$8.95
Nowhere to Run	Gay G. Gunn	$10.95

Object of His Desire	A. C. Arthur	$8.95
One Day at a Time	Bella McFarland	$8.95
Passion	T.T. Henderson	$10.95
Past Promises	Jahmel West	$8.95
Path of Fire	T.T. Henderson	$8.95
Picture Perfect	Reon Carter	$8.95
Pride & Joi	Gay G. Gunn	$8.95
Quiet Storm	Donna Hill	$8.95
Reckless Surrender	Rochelle Alers	$8.95
Rendezvous with Fate	Jeanne Sumerix	$8.95
Revelations	Cheris F. Hodges	$8.95
Rivers of the Soul	Leslie Esdaile	$8.95
Rooms of the Heart	Donna Hill	$8.95
Shades of Brown	Denise Becker	$8.95
Shades of Desire	Monica White	$8.95
Sin	Crystal Rhodes	$8.95
So Amazing	Sinclair LeBeau	$8.95
Somebody's Someone	Sinclair LeBeau	$8.95
Someone to Love	Alicia Wiggins	$8.95
Soul to Soul	Donna Hill	$8.95
Still Waters Run Deep	Leslie Esdaile	$8.95
Subtle Secrets	Wanda Y. Thomas	$8.95
Sweet Tomorrows	Kimberly White	$8.95
The Color of Trouble	Dyanne Davis	$8.95
The Price of Love	Sinclair LeBeau	$8.95
The Reluctant Captive	Joyce Jackson	$8.95
The Missing Link	Charlyne Dickerson	$8.95
Three Wishes	Seressia Glass	$8.95
Tomorrow's Promise	Leslie Esdaile	$8.95
Truly Inseperable	Wanda Y. Thomas	$8.95
Twist of Fate	Beverly Clark	$8.95
Unbreak My Heart	Dar Tomlinson	$8.95
Unconditional Love	Alicia Wiggins	$8.95
When Dreams A Float	Dorothy Elizabeth Love	$8.95

Whispers in the Night	Dorothy Elizabeth Love	$8.95
Whispers in the Sand	LaFlorya Gauthier	$10.95
Yesterday is Gone	Beverly Clark	$8.95
Yesterday's Dreams, Tomorrow's Promises	Reon Laudat	$8.95
Your Precious Love	Sinclair LeBeau	$8.95

ESCAPE WITH INDIGO !!!!

Join Indigo Book Club©
It's simple, easy and secure.

Sign up and receive the new releases
every month + Free shipping and
20% off the cover price.

Go online to www.genesis-press.com
and click on Bookclub or
call 1-888-INDIGO-1

Order Form

Mail to: Genesis Press, Inc.
P.O. Box 101
Columbus, MS 39703

Name _____

Address _____

City/State _____ Zip _____

Telephone _____

Ship to (if different from above)

Name _____

Address _____

City/State _____ Zip _____

Telephone _____

Credit Card Information

Credit Card # _____ ☐ Visa ☐ Mastercard

Expiration Date (mm/yy) _____ ☐ AmEx ☐ Discover

Qty.	Author	Title	Price	Total

Use this order form, or call
1-888-INDIGO-1

Total for books	_____
Shipping and handling: $5 first two books, $1 each additional book	_____
Total S & H	_____
Total amount enclosed	_____

Mississippi residents add 7% sales tax